Saying I Love You

New Adult Sweet Romance Series, Volume 2

Ellie J. Adams

Published by Wheelhouse Publishers LLC, 2020.

Copyright

Chapter 1

"Hey, Ashley, Mr. Handsome CEO at five o'clock," said Chelsea.

Mr. Handsome CEO, as Chelsea referred to him, was Brandon Mitchell, the 29-year-old CEO of Davenport Media. Davenport's flagship company was Jacqueline fashion magazine, founded by Brandon's grandmother Jacqueline Davenport. It was my dream to work at Jacqueline.

The Davenport family were also the primary benefactors of Davenport School of the Arts at Santa Barbara University. I recently graduated with a degree in Fashion Media from the school. I hoped it would give me a leg up in interviewing for the few entry-level positions available at Jacqueline this year.

I also hoped that helping with the evening's fundraiser for the school would increase my visibility. I did receive two complimentary tickets to the event. As I wasn't dating anyone at the moment, I brought Chelsea as my plus one.

"I have to admit, Ash, he is super handsome. Movie leading man handsome," Chelsea panted.

I whirled around. Brandon Mitchell was speaking with the president of the university and a few of the school's other top donors. His designer black tuxedo matched his short, dark hair and perfectly fit his tall, athletic frame. Even from a distance, it was obvious he was fit. He had the physique of a pro athlete more than a media mogul CEO.

His bronzed skin seemed more natural than the result of time in the sun or a tanning booth. He had a strong chin that accentuated his classic, handsome face. Chelsea was correct, Brandon Mitchell could easily be cast as a top leading-man in Hollywood. He was the epitome of tall, dark, and handsome.

His movements were smooth and controlled. Even from my vantage point I could tell that he was captivating those around him.

"So, are you going to talk to him?" asked Chelsea.

"What would I possibly say?"

"How about, 'Hello, my name is Ashley Sullivan, and I'd like you to hire me, marry me, and be the father of my children,'" Chelsea replied.

"Chels, seriously," I said as I playfully smacked her arm.

"Okay. Then let's devise your opening statement and closing argument. And remember, during conversation, never ask a question you don't know the answer to."

"Hold on there, Perry Mason, this isn't a trial."

Chelsea had graduated top of our class with a degree in Economics. In the fall she was starting law school at Columbia University.

Chelsea Richards had been my roommate and best friend since our freshman year at Santa Barbara University. She is smart as a whip, beautiful, playful, and an absolute doll. I lucked out in the roommate lottery. I couldn't hope for a better friend than Chelsea. I loved her like sister and would do anything for her.

"Okay. But you at least need to have some idea of what you would say to him. You're not just going to stare adoringly at him from across the room. I won't allow it."

"You won't allow it?"

"Ash, someone has make sure that you put yourself out there to land your dream job. You are much to talented and have worked much too hard not to get a job at Jacqueline. Besides, I want you to move to New York City. I don't want us living on separate coasts."

"I have the interview set up for tomorrow with a recruiter from Jacqueline. My portfolio is all ready to go. I'll dazzle them," I said.

"I know you will, Sweetie. Just sayin', can't hurt to make a good impression with Mr. Handsome CEO."

"I doubt he concerns himself with applicants for entry-level positions."

"Well, maybe he'll ask you out on a date," said Chelsea only half joking.

"Chels, get real."

"So, do you deny that Brandon Mitchell is an eligible bachelor?" said Chelsea using her best cross-examination voice.

"I didn't say that," I replied with a grin.

I didn't have much of a defense. Brandon Mitchell could date any woman he wanted. In fact, he has dated many of the most gorgeous women in the world. From supermodels to movie stars. He was once rumored to be an item with a stunning princess in Europe. Models, movie stars, and an actual princess!

"Nonetheless," I continued, "I hardly think Brandon Mitchell would have any interest in me."

"What?! You don't think you could get him?"

"Chelsea. It's not like I'm throwing some pity party here. All I am saying is it's not realistic to think that somebody like him would date someone like me. We're from two completely different worlds."

"Seriously, Ash. You look A-MA-ZING! Don't sell yourself short."

Chelsea meant well. And as brilliant and driven as she was, Chelsea had a playful side. She also tended to project her drop-dead gorgeous looks onto me.

Can I hold my own in picking up your average cute guy? I suppose. Not that I have dated much. A few boyfriends in high school and exactly two during college.

I don't exactly fit the mold of Brandon Mitchell's bevy of beauties. Chelsea, maybe. But I would give my chances of Brandon Mitchell even feigning interest in me at zero. As in zip, zilch, nada.

"Say, Ash?"

"Yeah?"

"Remember when I said you should think about what to say to Brandon Mitchell?"

"Sure, silly, it was only a few minutes ago."

"Well, you better think fast. He's heading our way."

"Shut up!"

"I'm serious."

And she was. Brandon Mitchell was on a direct path to where we were standing. Unless he veered off at the last second to take a dip in the fountain, it was hard to see where else he would be going.

I had little doubt he had noticed Chelsea and was going to ask her to dance. That is typically how an evening like this would go for us. I knew, however, she would decline and push me toward him. Chelsea is the most amazing friend and, at the moment, was only thinking of how this could benefit me.

"Remember to smile. You have a great smile," Chelsea advised. "And push your chest out a bit."

"Stop it! I'm nervous enough as is."

My entire body heated up as he got close. I was certain that my cheeks were flushed. My heart was racing and my palms were sweaty. I gave my right hand a quick wipe on my gown as he approached.

"Ms. Sullivan? I'm Brandon Mitchell," he said extending his hand. He is here to speak with me? Wait, . . . he knows who I am?

He was even more handsome up close. In fact, I was looking at the most handsome man I had ever seen. I couldn't imagine anyone more handsome. I couldn't think at all.

I shook his hand quickly before my sweaty palms returned. When our hands touched a wave of energy transferred between us. I Somehow managed to squeak out a response.

"Yes. Ashley Sullivan. Pleased to meet you, Mr. Mitchell."

"The pleasure is all mine. And, please, call me Brandon." His voice was deep and smooth. It had a rhythmic and hypnotic quality.

He was about six inches taller than me, but my heels gave me a little lift. I explored his face. His eyes were a gorgeous blue. Pictures I had seen of him didn't even come close to capturing how beautiful they were. That is saying a lot since they looked pretty spectacular in those pictures.

"Brandon, this is my best friend Chelsea Richards."

"Nice to meet you, Ms. Richards," he said politely, but then immediately returned his attention to me.

Whoa! That doesn't happen every day. That hasn't happened any day, at least not that I have ever seen. Even a man as handsome as Brandon Mitchell could see how stunning Chelsea was. I guess there is a first for everything.

"I understand that you are a top graduate of the Fashion Media program," Brandon said.

I watched the words form on his lips. Focus, Ashley. Focus.

"Um . . . Yes. I mean, I did just graduate with my bachelor's in Fashion Media. I guess I did okay in my classes."

"She's being modest," interjected Chelsea. "She had the highest GPA in her program and has an amazing portfolio of work."

"So, I hear," said Brandon.

I shot Chelsea a quick glance to cool it. I appreciated her enthusiasm and support, but I knew how she could get. I didn't want her overselling me.

"So, what are your plans now that you have graduated? Will we have the good fortune of you joining the fashion world in New York?" he asked with a broad smile.

I blushed. "I'm not quite sure, yet. I have a job offer at Adele in Los Angeles, but –"

"She has an interview tomorrow with your HR reps from Jacqueline," Chelsea offered. "If they're smart, they will hire her on the spot. You don't want to lose her to the competition."

So much for Chelsea not overselling.

Brandon tilted his head toward Chelsea and crossed his arms over his chest.

"You don't say," he replied. "Well, Ms. Richards, from what Ashley's professors have told me, I would tend to agree with you."

Chelsea flashed me a smug grin of satisfaction.

Brandon glanced down at his watch. He dropped his arms to his side and switched his gaze back toward me.

His dreamy blue eyes are looking straight at me. His strong, confident chin is pointing in my direction. His lovely lips are forming words directed at me. Wait! Oh, no! He's speaking to me! *Pay attention.*

"I have about fifteen minutes," he said. "Ashley, if you can spare the time, I'd love to chat a little more with you about your interest in Jacqueline."

I nodded. "Yes, of course."

"Excellent," he responded with a broad smile. His teeth were perfectly straight and a glistening white. "It was nice meeting you, Ms. Richards. If you will please excuse us. I'm going to steal your friend for a few moments."

"Steal away," she said. I detected a hint of satisfaction in her voice.

Brandon Mitchell placed his hand on the small of my back and I melted inside. He guided me toward the lobby and I felt like I was floating on air.

Chapter 2

"Do you mind if we get some fresh air?" he asked.

"Not at all. That would be nice."

Like a gentleman, he pushed open a front door of the arts building and allowed me to exit ahead of him. I caught his reflection in the glass. He was taking the opportunity to check out the way my gown showed off my backside.

I was trying not to read too much into it. The gown I was wearing was one of those outfits that could make pretty much any girl look great. Just an innocent little look. Then again, he seemed to have no reaction to Chelsea. Hmm.

Even if I got just the one look, it made my heart flutter. I'd need to thank Maria for picking the gown out for me. I worked part time at Maria's, a designer dress boutique in downtown Santa Barbara. As a perk, I get dresses from her 'Runway Rental' collection at 50% off.

The Narciso Rodriguez dress was the perfect combination of sophistication meets attractive. It was a black silk formal gown. Sleeveless with a square neckline.

There was a chill in the air and Brandon immediately removed his jacket and stepped toward me.

"As beautiful as you look in that dress, I think you are going to catch a cold if you don't cover up."

He placed his jacket over my shoulders. His arms came around me in one swift motion. A jolt of excitement shot down my spine. For that moment there was little space between us. My body tingled. His warm breath on my neck entranced me.

I somehow managed to whisper "Thank you, that is better."

I was now putting Brandon Mitchell's interest in me somewhere north of zero. How far north I wasn't quite sure. But we had crossed over from professional to something more.

He stepped back and perched himself against the stone wall next to the steps. He pursed his lips and let out a breath. "Ashley, I have a confession to make."

I tilted my head with intrigue. At this point, I was ready for him to say just about anything.

"I knew who you were before this evening. In fact, I've thoroughly reviewed your employment application."

Brandon was deliberate in what he said. Not rehearsed, nor forced, but he had a goal in mind and knew exactly how to present it.

"You will soon discover that I leave little to chance. At least, in so far as I can control a situation. I have to be that way to keep Davenport Media at the top of its game and one step ahead of the competition."

He paused for a moment. I was silent and attentive. I could tell that he still had more to say.

"Digital and social media has dramatically changed the fashion magazine industry. It will continue to do so. It's why this school is so important. It's why I need people like you working for me."

He stood and stepped toward me. He placed his hand on my arm. I nearly jumped. He captivated me like I never had been before.

"I know what people say about me . . . at least what the tabloids report. While exaggerated, it is not unfounded. But I am also a lot more. And I am looking for something more, something different in my life."

This had definitely taken a turn from professional. He was pivoting the conversation back to something more personal. He looked at me with determination.

Our eyes locked and his gaze entranced me. His gorgeous eyes sparkled as moonlight seemed to reflect off of them. His mouth turned up into a smile.

"Ashley, I can't explain it all to you tonight. But I am captivated by what little I know about you. When I saw your picture . . ."

He could see my raised eyebrow. He let out a nervous laugh. A slight chink in the armor.

"Oh that . . . I checked out your Facebook page," he admitted with some reluctance.

I'm not sure why he was hesitant to admit that. Many employers were now searching Facebook and other social media sites. A girl Chelsea and I knew had a job offer until HR found her tagged in pictures from one Spring Break.

My Facebook wall was pretty lame, so no concerns there. A few selfies of Chelsea and me at the beach was as racy as it got. I don't know why, but I blushed at the thought that Brandon saw a picture of me at the beach.

He picked up on my slight embarrassment.

"Don't worry, there was nothing disqualifying there. In fact, you are the exact person that I need working with me. But I don't have time to discuss details with you this evening."

He took my hand in his. Another wave of excitement washed over me. My knees began to feel like gelatin.

"Ashley, what I wanted you to know tonight is that I have an amazing position in mind for you at Jacqueline. I can explain it all to you tomorrow night."

Seems he had already decided on another meeting. He continued, "And the job offer will have nothing to do with anything else. Do you understand?"

"Yes, I think so."

"Good. Because I also want you to know that my interest in you extend beyond a job offer. I am attracted to you. I was from the moment I saw your picture. When I saw you tonight . . . when I saw you tonight, you took my breath away. You are stunning."

Beautiful. Stunning. Okay, we are now a healthy distance north of zero.

"Mr. Mitchell, –"

"Brandon," he reminded me.

"Brandon, I don't know what to say."

"Say that you will have dinner with me tomorrow night at Francesca's."

Francesca's was one of the finest restaurants in Santa Barbara. Very expensive and romantic. Or so I have heard.

"Yes. I would love to have dinner with you tomorrow night."

"Excellent! How is seven o'clock?"

"Perfect."

"Ashley, everything will become clearer tomorrow night. Are you still at the address on your application?"

"Yes. The apartment complex just off campus."

"Then I will pick you up at seven. Now, I should get you back to Chelsea. I'm sure she is anxious to know what we have been talking about."

"You have no idea. Oh, by the way, what should I do about the interview I have scheduled for tomorrow afternoon?"

"Don't worry about that. I'll have my executive assistant call HR and let them know that you are interviewing for another position. And that your interview will be with me."

He smiled. It was warm and comforting. I smiled back. Silence is golden. And my head was spinning.

What just happened? It seemed that my whole future changed in a few moments.

I was over the moon and I didn't know how I would get through the next day thinking about dinner with Brandon. Both an interview for my dream job and a date with my dream guy.

Somebody pinch me.

Chapter 3

"I have nothing to wear," I said as I flipped through the outfits in my closet. I could sense Chelsea rolling her eyes as she sat on my bed.

"Chels, don't roll your eyes at me."

"Who says I did?"

"Seriously?"

"Okay, okay. But, Ashley, Mr. Handsome CEO already is attracted to you. There are a dozen cute little numbers in your closet." She hopped off my bed and began flipping through my dresses.

"Normal cute. For a normal date. With a normal guy. Not Brandon Mitchell cute. Not for a date with him," I exclaimed.

"Do you even hear yourself? Ash, you are beautiful. What did he say? . . . Stunning!"

"Stunning in the 'Getting into Mischief Gown.'"

"What about this one?" Chelsea asked as she held up one of my best "date night" dresses.

"I wore that for Phil's birthday last year. Bad karma. I should give it away."

It had been six months since I broke up with my jerky ex-boyfriend, Phil. For me, that meant it had been six months since my last date.

I've heard people named Ashley have a deep inner desire for a stable, loving family or community. I think that is true of me. I had that growing up in my small town just outside of Austin, Texas. I knew that I wanted to get married and have a family. I also wanted a career in fashion media. A modern woman who would have it all.

"How about this?" Chelsea's voice snapped me back from my thoughts.

"Nope. Nothing in here will do. We need to make another trip to Maria's. We need to return our gowns from last night anyway," I stated.

"Are you crazy? You can't afford to rent a dress from Maria's every night. Besides, you don't need some fancy designer dress to impress anybody."

"First, it's not every night. Just last night and tonight. Second, with my employee's discount it is affordable."

Chelsea thought of protesting more, but I was already heading out of my bedroom. Last night's gowns in hand, I grabbed my car keys and purse off the kitchen counter.

"You coming?" I asked Chelsea.

"Yes," she replied, with some reluctance.

***

Fifteen minutes later we were at Maria's. Maria was a beautiful woman in her early 60's. She grew up in Italy and had been a model. Maria opened her dress shop over thirty years ago and has been a big part of the Santa Barbara community since.

"Ciao!" Maria greeted us as we entered the store.

"Ciao, Maria!" Chelsea and I replied.

"The gowns worked well for you two girls?" asked Maria as we handed the dresses to her.

"Yes. Thank you," I said.

"Worked great for Ashley. She has a date with Brandon Mitchell tonight," offered Chelsea.

"Well, part date and part business," I said.

"The Brandon Mitchell?" quizzed Maria, not seeming to hear what I had just said.

"Yes. Hard to believe, huh?" I answered.

"I think maybe he is a little like 'he who shall not be named'," said Maria. She was focusing like a laser beam on the date part and completely ignoring the job offer part.

"Maria, really?" I pleaded.

She grunted. Maria had become like a second mother to me. She knew all about Phil. Well, not everything. But enough. She was so disgusted by him that she liked to refer to him like he was Voldemort from the Harry Potter books.

"Not like Phil at all, Maria," I protested. Okay, Maria had a slight point. But there was something about Brandon that was different from Phil. And not just his success.

"Believe me, I learned my lesson. I'm more cautious now," I said as I looked at Chelsea for some back-up.

She looked at me like 'What do you want me to say?'

What? Now she has nothing to say?

"Look, I know Brandon's reputation. He's admitted some of it is true. He also said he is looking for something more now."

Maria just grunted again. Louder that time.

"I think this will be good for Ashley," volunteered Chelsea. Finally. Thank you.

"Until last night she had no relationship prospect on the horizon. Now she has a date with a successful and handsome man. It also sounds like she has an amazing job offer coming her way," she said.

"I at least want to explore all my options," I concluded.

"Bene, bene. Alright, alright. I can see that this is important to you. Besides, it is none of my business," said Maria.

"Oh, Maria. You know I love you and I value your opinion. You've been wonderful to me these past four years. But, yes, it is important to me," I said.

In that moment, Maria's expression changed. She even smiled.

"If you are happy about this, then I say 'Che meraviglia' . . . 'how wonderful.'"

I was relieved. Not that Maria was going to talk me out of dinner, and whatever else might happen. But I didn't want her upset either.

I took the opening she gave me.

"I was hoping you could help me find something for dinner at Francesca's."

"That is where Richie Rich is taking you?" Okay, so maybe Maria wasn't ready to drop it.

"Maria . . ." I whined.

"Va bene, okay, I'll let it go," she relented. Maria walked over to her Runway Rental dress rack. "Honey, I have just the dress. Now, it is not a dress that costs thousands like the ones that Mr. Mitchell's heiresses and starlets wear, but it looks like it. An exceptional dress," said Maria, now with a sense of conspiratorial satisfaction. "Besides, you are a pretty young woman. You don't even need an expensive designer dress to impress," she continued.

"That's what I said," Chelsea chimed in.

"Let's see the dress," I said as I pushed past Chelsea.

"It is a Parker Reina Dress. It retails for about $300, but rents for $40 a night. So, $20 for you. Just remember my little shop when you make it big in the fashion world."

"Oh, Maria, thank you!" I was giddy with excitement.

"Now, go try it on," said Maria as she pulled the dress off the rack and handed it to me.

I took the dress into the changing room and tried it on. I looked at myself in the mirror and beamed.

The silver metallic lace dress was the perfect mix of feminine and flirty. A sleeveless, V-neckline, racer back, pencil skirt.

"Come out. Let's see!" shouted Chelsea. She couldn't help herself. Chelsea had resigned herself to the fact that I was renting this dress. Besides, she couldn't argue that $20 was a great deal.

I swung open the changing room door and strutted across the store like a runway model. I did a twirl and giggled.

"Magnifico. Molto sexy!" exclaimed Maria.

"What she said," commented Chelsea.

"I'll take it!" I said.

I felt sophisticated and pretty. I felt ready for a date with Brandon Mitchell.

Chapter 4

Oh no! It's almost seven o'clock!

I put on a Cleopatra inspired gold-plated necklace with crystal detailing. It complimented the dress perfectly. Maria threw in the necklace rental for free. I'm not sure that our deal helped her bottom line, but it sure helped me. Despite her little protest, Maria was fabulous.

I checked myself in the mirror.

"Very cute!" said Chelsea as she walked into my room.

"You really think so?"

"I know so. Ash, you are super cute."

Right at seven the doorbell rang. Punctual.

I headed for the front door and peered out of the peep hole. My pulse quickened as I saw those unmistakable gorgeous blue eyes looking straight ahead. I unlatched the locks and opened the door.

"Good evening," said Brandon as he handed me a dozen red roses.

"Hi. Thank you. They're beautiful," I said as my cheeks turned the color of the roses.

"You're welcome. And they fail in comparison to the beauty before me. Ashley, you are gorgeous."

"Um, thanks." Okay, now I was two shades of red darker than the roses. "You look dashing."

That was the understatement of the century. Brandon looked more handsome than the night before. I hadn't thought that was even possible.

He was wearing an Armani suit. His broad shoulders were strong and confident. His bronze skin was smooth and clean shaven. He smelled delicious.

"Let me just put these in some water," I said carrying the bouquet into the kitchen.

"Here, let me take care of those," said Chelsea walking into the living room. "Hello, Mr. Mitchell. Nice to see you."

"Hi Chelsea. Please, call me Brandon."

"Thanks, Chels," I said as I handed the roses to her.

"Now, you kids have fun," Chelsea said.

"Okay. We will. What time is her curfew?" asked Brandon.

"She's a big girl. I'll let her decide what her curfew is."

"Are you two finished?" I asked.

"Yes, ma'am," said Brandon. "Shall we go?"

He held out his arm. I looped my arm through and we left. I could feel Chelsea's smile that stretched ear to ear. I knew how she felt.

Brandon escorted me to a luxury sports car. One of those two-seaters. He opened the passenger door, and I slid into the soft leather seat.

"It's a great night. After dinner maybe we'll put the top down," he said just before he shut the door. He climbed in on the driver's side and started the car. The engine hummed, and we were off.

"Nice car," I said. I realized it was an understatement.

"Thanks. It's an Aston Martin DB8. It's my California cruising car," he said with boyish enthusiasm. It was cute that he thought an Aston Martin DB8 meant something to me. I'm pretty girly. I didn't know the difference between an Aston Martin and Dean Martin.

Wait! Doesn't James Bond drive an Aston Martin? Yes. I think so. That little nugget of information got stored somewhere in the recesses of my mind. My dad loved the James Bond movies. I'd seen every one of them with him, at least once. I'm pretty sure about this. Let's find out.

"Hmm. Doesn't James Bond drive an Aston Martin?"

I thought Brandon was going to jump out of his seat with excitement. It must be a universal guy thing. I hadn't met a man yet who doesn't love James Bond. James Bond, and the Three Stooges.

"Yes. An Aston Martin DB5. Built between 1963 and 1965. I'd love to pick one up at an auction someday," he said.

"Any DB5? Or one used in the James Bond movies?" I asked.

"Any DB5 would be nice to have in a car collection. But I'd love one from the movies. That would make it extra special." He glanced over at me and smiled again. He had an exquisite smile. It was friendly and inviting.

I was going to enjoy learning more about this man. Brandon versus Phil. Not the same at all. Not even close.

"Did you know that each Aston Martin is hand built in England?" he said.

I didn't, but that wasn't the point. Again, cute that he would think that I had any idea.

"They are individually inspected at the factory," he continued. "The engine block has the inspector's name stamped on it."

"That's interesting. How long does it take to build each car?"

His nose scrunched and forehead wrinkled. I was seeing a whole other side of 'Mr. Handsome CEO.' Totally adorable.

"I don't know," he admitted. "That's an excellent question." He was beaming.

"Well, I appreciate the time they took. It is quite an exhilarating ride," I said.

"Ms. Sullivan, you are an amazing woman."

Brandon looked completely at ease behind the wheel. I couldn't believe I was sitting next to him in his car.

Yes, there was an attraction to his image in magazines and on television. Yes, I had innocent thoughts about him before we ever met. And, yes, the idea of being on an actual date with him, even if it included a business component, was thrilling beyond words.

I knew that I could enjoy this date to the fullest, but I also had to remember that it was my opportunity to land my dream job. I needed to at least get through dinner being able to hold a coherent conversation.

I needed to distract myself from thinking about Brandon as my date and more as my potential employer. This was going to test my mental strength. It was going to require a monumental feat of willpower.

Nails on a chalkboard . . . no . . . think. . .think . . .Got it!

"So, which one of the Three Stooges is your favorite?" I asked.

Brandon's face indicated that I had once again tapped into his inner boy. Mission accomplished. For now.

Chapter 5

Francesca's was exquisite with an elegant and romantic atmosphere. I was gobbed-struck by the large chandelier that hung in the center of the restaurant. Impressive works of fine art adorned the walls. The sight was only matched by the wonderful aromas that filled the air from its signature dishes.

Francesca's was a Michelin three-star restaurant located on the property of the Lusso Beach Resort & Spa. Lusso was a five-star resort on the Santa Barbara waterfront. Francesca's and Lusso epitomized the "American Riviera" vibe often identified with Santa Barbara. I could only dream of being able to afford a meal at the restaurant. A night's stay at the resort was even further beyond my budget.

Brandon took my hand as the hostess led us to a table with a panoramic view of the Pacific Ocean. The table was romantic with fresh-cut flowers and candlelight. I didn't know if this type of experience was in my future or not. I was taking it all in – carpe diem.

The waiter came and took our drink order. Brandon and I discussed what looked especially good on the menu. We ordered when our waiter came back with our drinks. I was taking in the view of the ocean.

Brandon spoke after the waiter left. "I think this is one of the most spectacular views in Santa Barbara."

"I agree. Thank you for taking me to dinner here this evening."

"It is my pleasure. I hope you like the food."

"Are you kidding? I've always wanted to eat here. I'm pretty sure it is going to be the best meal that I have ever had in my life."

"Well, I want tonight to be memorable for you."

"It already it is," I said.

"Don't you just love the way the ocean looks when it is so calm and peaceful?" Brandon asked.

"Yes. The way it reflects the moonlight. It has a magical quality to it," I replied as I gazed back out over the Pacific through the window.

"Magical is just the word I was thinking of describing you," Brandon said as he took my hand in his.

I turned to look at him. The reflection of candlelight danced in his eyes. Oh, those dreamy blue eyes!

He leaned forward. "Ashley, you look radiant and I'm finding it hard to concentrate on anything but you. I invited you to dinner this evening so that we could get to know one another on a personal level. Nonetheless, I also promised to explain my professional intentions."

I nodded.

"Why don't we get business out of the way so we can enjoy the rest of our evening," he continued as he gave my hand a light squeeze and then let go.

"Okay. I have to admit that I have been more than a little curious, and a bit anxious, after what you said last night," I replied.

"Well, I understand your curiosity. But, let me assure you, there is nothing to be anxious about. This will be the easiest job interview of your life. It's not even an interview. It is more my opportunity to explain my offer," Brandon said as he sat back, like I imagined he did in so many business meetings. He thought for a moment and then spoke again.

"I'm sure that your offer from Adele is quite adequate for someone just out of college. But I'm positive that any offer from Jacqueline will surpass it. It will also provide greater opportunity in the long run. Nonetheless, what I have in mind is even better than that."

Just then the waiter approached out table.

"Dinner will be out in just a few minutes. May I refresh your drinks for you?" asked the waiter as he presented the bottle of wine.

"Yes, please," Brandon replied.

The waiter refilled our glasses.

"May I get you anything else?" he asked after pouring the wine.

"No, thank you," Brandon said.

The waiter departed.

Brandon picked up with his train of thought from before the waiter had stopped by our table.

"I mentioned last night how impressed I was with your job application. When I read it, I knew that it would be a waste of your talents to hire you into an entry-level position. There are many excellent candidates that can fill those jobs. But the position that I have in mind requires an exceptional candidate. I am convinced that exceptional candidate is you, Ashley."

"Thank you. But, I . . . I don't know if I would consider myself exceptional," I replied.

"That may be your only weakness," Brandon said. "You underestimate yourself. Granted, there is a fine line between confidence and arrogance. I'm sometimes accused of the latter.

But, it is essential that an employee at Jacqueline always be confident. I especially expect that of those who work with me."

At that point I wasn't quite sure where Brandon was going with this. I think that he sensed that I was getting a bit uneasy. He seemed masterful at reading people. No doubt a key trait that fueled his success.

"Don't worry, Ashley. You are amazing. I wish I only had one weakness, and one so minor as yours," he said to reassure me.

"Now who is underestimating themselves?" I said trying to keep it light enough so I could control my nerves.

"Touché. Look, I just want you to know that you should not hold back. You have immense talent and instincts that will serve you, me, and Jacqueline well. Projecting a little more confidence and assertiveness will carry you, and us, a long way."

"Okay. Noted. Be more confident and assertive," I said.

I decided to put it to the test.

"Now, if you don't mind, I've been dying to know what sort of position you have in mind."

"There you go," Brandon said with a warm chuckle.

"Well, Mr. Mitchell . . .," I said as I reached for my glass and took a sip of wine.

"I think I could get use to the confident and assertive Ashley Sullivan. Okay, I won't keep you in suspense any longer. I had decided a few months ago that we needed to step up our game with digital social media. My grandmother built the magazine, but I am charged with keeping it edgy and relevant in the 21st century," he said.

"And you lack any significant digital social media presence," I offered. Of course that was no epiphany. It was clear to everyone that Jacqueline only had the most basic website and social media pages.

"Exactly. I have taken steps to remedy that. We have hired a new web development company and plan to add a social media team. We will curate our print material online to deliver digital editions. We will also offer new, interactive online content. What I have been lacking is someone who can head the efforts. That is, until I learned of you."

I couldn't believe what I was hearing. Well, I completely got what Brandon wanted to do. From a media perspective, I couldn't agree more. I was still in a bit of shock that he seemed to be indicating that the position he had in mind for me was heading a major department at the magazine.

"So . . . am I –?"

"Yes, Ashley. I am offering you the job."

"I'm flattered. I am, but Brandon –"

"But, nothing. Ashley, I saw the case study you designed for just this type of situation. It ran circles around any proposal I received from so-called 'experts' with years more experience than you have. I know a perfect match when I see it. This is a perfect fit for you," Brandon stated.

"It's a big job. I, I just don't –" I stammered.

"Alright, what happened to confident and assertive Ashley? Please send her back. Yes, it's a big job. But you can do it."

"I appreciate that you think that about me," I said.

"I don't think it. I know it. Besides, I also need someone with your media savvy who I would be happy to spend a lot of my time with. The position also requires establishing and managing my personal social media accounts. In many ways I am becoming the face of Jacqueline. I need to be more engaged to keep our readers more engaged."

"That is a trend with many CEO's. Especially in the fashion and media industries," I said.

"True. See, you have your pulse on what's needed right now. That is worth its weight in gold. Believe me. And speaking of monetary value, I have neglected to tell you the compensation package . . ."

Brandon told me the salary. I was certain my jaw hit the table and my tongue was hanging out. I couldn't believe it. I figured it would take me many years to even come close to what he told me I would make my first year.

"Plus," he continued, "you will have a full benefits package. It includes health, dental, vision, a matching 401k plan, and a month of vacation. I'm also including a generous expense account to cover outfits and entertaining. We are in the fashion business after all. We need to dress to impress and throw lavish parties now and then."

"Brandon, that is more than generous. I . . . I don't know what to say."

"Say that you will take the job."

"Yes! Of course, yes! I will take the job!"

I was on cloud nine about the job. It was beyond my wildest dreams. But then, I remembered it was merely a pre-cursor to an actual date with this man. Brandon had a look of bemusement and, well . . . I'd say a bit smitten.

"We'll work out the details tomorrow. The rest of tonight is about us," he said taking my hand once again. He gazed into my eyes and my heart skipped a beat.

"Ashley, I find you intoxicating. I want to discover what there may be for us beyond a work relationship."

His voice was soft and smooth. The temperature in the room seemed to rise by a hundred degrees. The waiter arrived with our meals. We enjoyed more casual conversation while we ate. We shared stories about our childhood.

Brandon grew up in Manhattan but spent a significant amount of time in Santa Barbara where his mother's family was from. He had also attended the finest boarding schools and traveled the world. He displayed business smarts at a young age and knew that he wanted to head the company one day. That came sooner than expected when his father decided to take an early retirement.

I shared how different my childhood was growing up in a small town outside of Austin. I expressed how happy my childhood was. I had also been fascinated by fashion and media. I had an eye for style and proved to be an excellent writer.

When I discovered the Fashion Media degree at Santa Barbara University, I knew that is where I wanted to attend college. I received funding from the Davenport School of the Arts scholarship fund and that made my dream a reality. Now, I was poised for a dream job at Jacqueline.

As we finished dinner, and the waiter cleared the table we peeked at the dessert menu.

"I really shouldn't. I need to watch my girlish figure," I said.

Brandon looked at me over the menu and said, "I don't think you have anything to worry about."

"You say that, but do you know how hard it is to work off the calories of one of these desserts?"

"You'll just need to get plenty of exercise later," he said with a devilish grin.

"Really? What did you have in mind?"

"A few laps around the resort should do the trick." Then he lowered the menu to see my reaction.

"Lucky you are so handsome," I finally said.

We decided on splitting a dessert. I was glad we went for dessert because it was out of this world. I was also glad that we split it. I didn't want to have to cut myself out of the dress.

"Dinner was wonderful. Thank you," I said as we got up from the table after Brandon paid the check. We crossed the restaurant arm-in-arm and I couldn't have been happier with the evening.

"I'd hate for our evening to end so soon. Would you like to take a stroll along the beach?" asked Brandon as we exited the restaurant.

"I'd love that. I Can burn off a few of the calories from dinner," I replied.

"Great. Although, let's take a leisurely stroll. I wouldn't want to exert too much energy."

Brandon gave me a peck on the cheek and I was over the moon.

He moved his arm around my shoulders and I leaned into him as we walked along a path from Francesca's to the beach. The stars were shining bright in the California night sky and the waves of the Pacific gently lapped the shore.

We walked and talked effortlessly for another hour. After he drove me home and asked if he could kiss me goodnight. I nodded sheepishly. He leaned in and we shared a soft and sweet kiss.

We said good night, and I entered my apartment. As I closed the door behind me, I couldn't stop smiling. What an evening it had been.

Chapter 6

It was amazing how much the past twenty-four hours had changed my life. I went from a hopeful college graduate to having a fabulous new career and starting a relationship with the man of my dreams.

"How did last night go?" asked Chelsea when she woke. "I tried to stay up last night, but finals week and graduation caught up with me. I was asleep by nine."

"No worries," I replied. "Even though I was excited, I didn't want to wake you. You were sleeping so peacefully."

"So how did it go?" Chelsea asked again, with even more excitement.

"Beyond anything I could have imagined." I told Chelsea about my dinner with Brandon, the new job, our walk on the beach, and the sweet kiss good night. "And he wants me to fly me up the coast for our second date."

"When?" Chelsea said.

"Today," I said.

"Everything is happening so fast," Chelsea said as she followed me down the hall.

"I know. I can hardly believe it. I told myself that I should have you pinch me to make sure I'm not dreaming. But, a simple verbal confirmation will due."

"You're not dreaming. I'm just wondering if it is all too good to be true. I mean, don't get me wrong, I'm thrilled for you and Mr. Handsome CEO –"

"Yes. It is all happening fast. But it feels right. The job will be amazing. The money even more amazing. And Brandon is the best part of all. Oh, Chels, I think I am in love!"

"I know I joke around a lot. I also admit that I encouraged you to put yourself out there. And, let's face it, I'm the last one who should talk when it comes to falling for a guy . . . "

"All true."

"But to say you are in love after one date? Ashley, slow down."

"I thought you would be happier. I got the job and the man. Plus we get to stay roommates. Just in New York City."

"Yes. I'm happy about all of it. I just didn't think things would happen this fast. I want to make sure that you don't get hurt. Are you sure the job doesn't have strings attached? Are you prepared for the possibility that you are just another date for him?"

Chelsea made some good points. All things I had considered. Okay, considered was too strong a word. The thoughts had entered my mind though. A little.

"For once, Chels, I'm going with what feels right. I'm not going to over-analyze this like I do most things. Brandon and I are going to take the relationship part as it unfolds. As far as the job . . . I'd never get anything better."

Chelsea was silent.

"Come on, Chels.

Our doorbell rang.

"Can you get it? I need to get dressed," I said as I looked through my dresser.

"Sure. But we still need to talk about this. I need more details," she replied as she turned to go answer the door.

I could hear Brandon and Chelsea exchanging pleasantries as she opened the door. It sounded like she was on her best behavior. I finished dressing and headed into the living room.

"There. I'm all set and ready to go," I announced.

I knew that Chelsea wanted some reassurances. "Let's plan on a girls day out tomorrow," I said as I gave Chelsea a hug. "How about a day at the spa? My treat."

"That sounds great, but –"

I stopped her before she could ask if I could afford it.

"Chels. Don't worry about it. Thanks to my great new job I can afford it and I want to do this. It will be my way of celebrating with my best friend."

"Okay. Just don't go spending all your money before you've earned your first paycheck," she said.

"I won't. You can put your economics degree to use and help me plan out my budget. I'll text you later once I have things set for tomorrow."

"Have a safe trip," she said as Brandon opened the door.

"We will. See you tomorrow," I said as I went out the door.

"See you later," Brandon said to Chelsea as he followed me out into the hallway.

As the door closed behind us Brandon turned to me.

"Is Chelsea okay?" he asked.

"She will be. There is a lot of big changes all at once. When I have time to discuss it all with her everything will be fine," I said as I took Brandon by the hand and we walked out to his car.

It was such a nice day that Brandon had the top down on the Aston Martin. I had put my hair into a pony tail and was wearing a pink Santa Barbara University baseball cap. Brandon put a New York Yankees cap on his head. He reached down onto the center console for his sunglasses and checked his look in the side mirror before he started the car.

I didn't want to tell Brandon that my Dad grew up in Maine and was a Red Sox fan.

Plenty of time for that later.

"Ready to go?" he asked.

"All set," I said as we both clicked our seat belts in place.

It was a quick ride to the airport. There was a separate entrance that led to a series of private hangers for corporate and charter jets. Brandon parked in the hanger and we got out.

Two men in pilot's uniforms greeted us. Brandon introduced them as the pilot and co-pilot. A woman emerged from the plane's cabin.

"Good afternoon, Mr. Mitchell," she said as she stepped off the steps of the plane.

"Good afternoon, Linda. This is Ms. Ashley Sullivan. She is our new Director of Digital and Social Media."

"A pleasure to meet you, Ms. Sullivan," said Linda. "Should you need anything in flight, please don't hesitate to let me know."

"Thank you," I said.

Brandon took my hand and led me up the short steps into the cabin of the plane. I wasn't sure if anyone noticed that Brandon took me by the hand. I suppose they could have figured he was being a gentleman and helping me up the steps.

Perhaps they didn't notice. Perhaps it wasn't their business to notice, or care. It did get me thinking about how we were going to handle the business and personal aspects of our relationship. I was also thinking more about what Chelsea had said to me earlier that morning.

The cabin of the jet smelled of leather and polished wood. There were six large leather seats. They looked more like living room recliners than airplane seats. Between two of the seats was a shiny wood table. There was also a leather couch that seated three.

Brandon escorted me to one of the seats at the table. He sat in the seat opposite me.

"Once we're at cruising altitude, Linda will get us lunch," he said.

"This is nice," I said looking around the plane. I was saying that a lot lately.

"Get's us where we need to go," said Brandon as he tapped out a text message on his iPhone. "Much more convenient than flying commercial."

He powered off his phone and placed it in his back pocket. I figured even though it was a private flight that the same rules applied about electronic devices. I pulled my phone out of my purse and powered it off.

"After we eat do you want to take a look at some New York apartments online? I can connect you with my real estate agent and he can help you find a great place."

"Um . . . Yes, I suppose," I replied. Brandon's question caught me a bit off guard.

I would certainly need to find a place to live. But in that moment, it became another new thing. Another change that was coming fast.

"Is everything okay? You don't sound excited about the idea of apartment hunting."

Before I had a chance to answer, the flight crew boarded the plane.

"We just need to finish our pre-flight check in the cockpit and then we'll be ready to get under way," the pilot announced to Brandon.

"How does the flight look to be shaping up?" Brandon asked.

"Clear skies and calm. Should be a smooth flight," the pilot answered. "I'll give you an update once we reach cruising altitude."

He and the co-pilot continued into the cockpit and Linda pulled the cabin door shut. She sat in one of the seats at the rear of the plane. The pilot announced that we should fasten our seat belts and prepare for take off.

A truck pulled the plane out of the hanger and then the engines roared to life. After a few minutes of taxiing, our jet accelerated down the runway and we took off. I peered out the window as Santa Barbara became smaller as we climbed into the sky. Once we leveled off, Linda got up and served us drinks and then went to the galley to prepare our lunch.

"So, you didn't have a chance to answer my question," Brandon said once Linda was in the galley.

"Oh, right... I'm fine. Maybe I'm just starting to feel a little overwhelmed. So much is happening. Just a few days ago I was a recent college graduate and now I have a new career, a new city, I'm on a private corporate jet with the CEO, and . . ."

I leaned over the table and lowered my voice to a whisper, "there's whatever is happening between us."

"I guess when you put it that way," he said rubbing his chin, "it is a lot to process. I'm so used to charging forward and acting fast to get things done, that I forget not everyone moves at my speed."

"Well, it's not just that," I said as I looked over my shoulder. I was pretty sure that Linda couldn't make out what we were saying, but I didn't want to take any chances.

"Maybe we should talk about this later," I concluded.

"If it's privacy you're concerned about, I can assure you that the crew pays no attention –"

"It is private," I interjected. I realized there was an edge to my voice. Brandon also noticed.

"Fine. We can talk after lunch. Linda has noise canceling headphones she can wear from her seat at the back of the jet. Will that provide enough privacy for you?"

"Yes. And you don't need to take that tone with me," I replied. I was hoping this wasn't turning into our first argument.

"You're right. I'm sorry. I just don't know what is troubling you."

Linda emerged from the galley with our lunch. Brandon and I ate in silence. I did enjoy the food. I don't know why I was so surprised, given the luxury of the jet, but the food was much better than I expected.

After we finished eating, Linda cleared our dishes. She checked to see if we wanted anything else and then sat in her seat at the back of the cabin. She pulled on her headphones, opened up a book, and began reading.

I guess Linda was used to Brandon conducting sensitive business during flights. It was either understood she was wear to the headphones, or she just felt more comfortable doing so. I didn't ask which it was.

"Is it safe to speak?" asked Brandon gently to break the ice.

"Yes. I'm sorry. Brandon, these are big changes for me. I have been so caught up in the whirlwind of the past few days. I haven't had much time to think about how much is changing."

"Okay. And now you are starting to think about it. How can I help?"

The intercom crackled for a few seconds.

"Hold that thought," Brandon said.

"Mr. Mitchell," the Pilot's voice came over the intercom, "we have a good tailwind. We are looking to arrive ten minutes ahead of schedule. I'll let you know when we are about to begin our approach into the airport." The intercom went silent again.

"So, talk to me Ashley. What do we need to work through?"

"I don't know that it's that straightforward. I'm not sure there is a problem, per se, to work through. Something Chelsea said this morning has me thinking."

"What did Chelsea say?"

"She just wondered if it is all to good to be true. You have to admit that it could look that way. A fabulous new job, an amazing date, a quick trip up the coast on the private corporate jet . . ."

"I've already explained why I sought you out for the job. Jacqueline provides generous compensation packages to hire and retain the best in the industry. Your salary is not out of line with positions of equal responsibility. I've tried my best to express my attraction to you. I'll let last night speak for itself."

"Yes. I know that. I appreciate what went on in screening my application. I understand the thought that went into making a decision to hire me. I'm happy to have the position, and the salary, and I know I will do a great job to earn it. As for last night, it was amazing. The best date of my life."

"Then what, exactly, is the problem, Ashley?"

"If last night was the start of something, how do we handle it?"

"In what way?"

"At work, for starters?"

"We each have our jobs to do. We will conduct them with the utmost professionalism. I won't show favoritism when it comes to making business decisions. People will find out about us. I don't care. You shouldn't either. We can have both a successful professional and personal relationship if we work at it. I try not to complicate things."

Everything Brandon said made sense to me. I understood what he was saying and couldn't find any disagreement with it. Chelsea was still in my head. She was there because I wanted her to be there.

"Chelsea doesn't want to see me get hurt. I don't want to get hurt either."

"Hurt by what? Your dream job? A more than generous salary? All expenses paid travel? Dating me? Tell me what could harm you in any of that?" Brandon's voice now had an edge to it. He seemed affronted. He wasn't happy with direction of the conversation.

I looked into Brandon's eyes. Those amazing blue eyes that so captivated my attention. Those blue eyes that could reach deep inside and make be feel pure joy. In that moment they did none of those things. They were angry.

"By you. Hurt by you," I finally said.

"By me?! Look, Ashley, I told you that I can't make any promises about where this is all going. If you're honest, neither can you. One step at a time. Remember? But I'm not out to hurt you. You believe me, right?"

I nodded my head.

"Ashley, I need to hear you say it." The edge was gone in his voice, but there was still a seriousness to his tone.

"Yes. I believe you."

While it had been less than 48 hours since I first met Brandon in person, he hadn't given me a reason not to believe him. I couldn't deny what he said about my job at Jacqueline. It wouldn't make any business sense to pursue and hire me if he didn't believe I was the right person for the job.

I also couldn't deny my attraction to him. Nor did he need to be with me if he didn't have a similar attraction.

"So, are we good?" Brandon asked, wanting to be done with the conversation.

"We're good," I said as I put my hand on his.

"I like the sound of that."

"Why don't we take a look and get some ideas about where I might live," I said.

"Alright, then," he said as he took out his iPad. The glimmer was back in his eyes. It was so easy to get lost in his eyes and how handsome he was. I didn't think I could ever get tired of looking into his eyes.

Chapter 7

Brandon and I strolled around San Francisco for the afternoon and enjoyed a casual dinner before returning to Santa Barbara. A great second date, which ended with another sweet kiss at my front door.

I kept my promise to Chelsea, and we had a wonderful spa day just for the girls the following afternoon. We talked, and she was more comfortable about my new job. She even felt better that I had spoken with Brandon about our situation. She jumped out of her chair when I showed her some of the apartments I was considering in Manhattan.

She was over the moon that we would be rooming together. She had a hard time accepting that she wouldn't need to pay rent, but was appreciative. Chelsea was a realist and knew that her financial aid would go much further without having to pay rent. We agreed that she could chip in toward utilities and food.

I called my family and told them about my new job and move to New York. I left out any mention of Brandon beyond the job offer. It was much too soon.

I knew how my mother was. She'd want to know all about him and how serious it was. I told them that I would be home for Thanksgiving.

I visited with Maria to say goodbye. She told me it wasn't "addio" ("goodbye") but, rather, "arrivederci" ("see you later"). She also reminded me not to forget her little dress boutique when I made it big in the fashion world.

I had one day to pack before Brandon and I left for New York. Chelsea was staying in Santa Barbara until our lease ended in August. I told her I would write her a check to cover my half of the remaining rent as soon as I got my first paycheck.

"I can't believe you only have one day to pack," Chelsea said as she helped me pull my large suitcase down from the closet.

"Well, this apartment came furnished. So I am only packing clothes and belongings. I don't have that much."

"I'm going to miss you," said Chelsea with sadness in her voice.

"It's only two months, then we'll be roomies again. Except in New York City."

"I know. It will all be different though."

"Don't get all sentimental on me. You know I'm a big baby and cry at the drop of a hat," I reminded her.

"I'll try."

"Yes. It will be different. But it is a new adventure. We'll still be us and we'll have fun. Just like always," I said as I wrapped my arms around Chelsea for a hug. "Now, help me pack," I said.

We finished packing and ordered takeout from our favorite Chinese restaurant. We talked, and laughed, and cried about our four years at Santa Barbara University. I was looking forward to talking, and laughing, and even crying, with Chelsea in New York. Life was better with my BFF.

Morning came and Brandon and I took the company jet cross country. The view of the New York skyline was spectacular as we approached the airport. Brandon pointed out various landmarks.

After we had landed and pulled into a private hanger at the airport, Brandon escorted me to the company helicopter waiting on the nearby runway. We flew to Davenport Media headquarters. The view of the skyline was even more spectacular from the helicopter. It was all so surreal.

We landed on the roof of the building and the rotors of the helicopter slowed. The man who guided the helicopter onto the landing pad opened the door to the helicopter. Brandon stepped out and then took my hand and assisted me out.

"Good evening, Mr. Mitchell," the man shouted over the engine as it whined down.

"Good evening, Ray." Brandon didn't bother introducing me over the noise.

"Welcome to New York, Ms. Sullivan," Brandon said to me with a smile.

"Why, thank you, Mr. Mitchell."

Brandon bit his lip, took in a breath and then exhaled.

"I hate to do this to you on your first night in the city . . ."

"What is it?"

"I'm leaving in fifteen minutes for Toronto. I have an early morning meeting and it makes more sense to fly up there tonight. The good news is that I will be back tomorrow afternoon."

I pouted and then kissed him on the cheek.

"It's okay. I understand. Besides, I'll want to get a good night sleep before my first day tomorrow."

"And don't worry about tomorrow," he said. "It will just be filling out forms for payroll, meeting some of the staff, and getting settled into your new office."

I hadn't even thought about exactly where I was going to be working.

"I get an office?" I asked with glee.

"For my Director of Digital and Social Media? Of course. It's not huge, but it has a pretty nice view. And, it has a prime location in the building."

"Where's that?"

"Just down the hall from my office."

"Ooh! I like the sound of that. Just try to avoid the pop-in, or I won't get anything done," I said as I rested my head against his chest.

"The great thing about being the CEO, is that I can pop-in whenever I want and no one can say anything about it. Including you," Brandon said as he kissed me on top of my head.

I looked up at him.

"Brandon, I don't want special treatment. And I don't want people talking more than they already will. I want to be taken seriously for my work. I want to do a great job for the company."

"And you will. Don't worry. If anything, we'll be lucky to be able steal even a few minutes alone together during the day."

"And after hours?"

"As much as possible."

"Good."

"Before I forget, I had my assistant book you into a hotel for the evening. The car service will take you there tonight and pick you up from the hotel in the morning."

"You're sweet."

"I want this to be as stress free as possible."

"And you feel a little guilty about leaving me all alone my first night in New York?" I teased.

"That, too. Oh, by the way, how about dinner tomorrow evening at Tavern on the Green, followed by a carriage ride through Central Park? A New York experience I want you to have as soon as possible."

"Sounds amazing. I can't wait."

"Neither can I." Brandon gave me a peck on the cheek. "Have a great night and I will see you tomorrow."

With my own kiss to Brandon, I smiled and wrapped my arms around him. "Have a safe trip. See you tomorrow."

We hugged for a moment and then Brandon turned and headed back toward the helicopter. I got on the elevator and made my way to the first floor, through lobby, and to the waiting car. Brandon had booked me a room at the Four Seasons and I enjoyed a decadent and relaxing evening.

I drifted off to sleep and dreamed of Brandon and the start of my new life in New York City.

Chapter 8

It was a beautiful spring morning in New York. I thought about how pleasant it should be for the carriage ride through Central Park later that evening. I was enjoying sitting in the back of the Towne Car as the driver maneuvered through the heavy city traffic. My cell phone buzzed. It was Brandon.

"Hi, how is Toronto?" I said as I answered his call.

"Fine. One meeting down and another to go. I just wanted to call and wish you luck for your first morning at the office."

"Thank you. That is sweet of you. I'm in the car now and should be there in a few minutes."

"Excellent. Teresa, my executive assistant, will be waiting for you in the lobby. She'll help you get settled in. Don't hesitate to ask her for anything you may need."

"Do most new employees get this kind of treatment?"

There was a slight pause on the other end of the phone.

"No. But you're not most new employees. You are part of the executive team and . . . "

"Okay, okay. I'll let it go. Besides, I have to admit that the treatment is nice."

"I've got to run. Have a great morning and I'll see you this afternoon."

"See you this afternoon. Bye."

As I put my phone back in my purse I was thinking about how amazing this all was. I hoped that it wasn't to good to be true. I didn't have much time to think any more about it as the car pulled up in front of the Davenport building. The driver got out and opened my door.

"Have a wonderful day, Ms. Sullivan," he said.

"Thank you. I hope you have a wonderful day as well."

"I'll have your luggage sent up to your office."

"Thank you."

I crossed the sidewalk and entered the building through the revolving door. The lobby glistened with marble. Employees scurried toward the bank of elevators.

"Ms. Sullivan," I heard a woman's voice call to me.

As I turned I saw an attractive young woman approach me. She was a few inches taller than I was and I guessed only a few years older. She could give Chelsea a run for her money in the beauty department. I wasn't happy with the realization that she was probably Brandon's executive assistant.

"Ms. Sullivan, I'm Teresa Barnes," she said as she extended her hand.

Dammit. I immediately wondered if Brandon had ever had sex with her. Unlike last night, where the number of anonymous women was a turn on, I felt a pang of jealousy. Then I put it out of my head. At this point, did it matter?

"Hello. Nice to meet you," I said as I shook her hand.

"I'll be assisting you this morning. Help you find your way around, get your paperwork processed, and do my best to answer any questions you may have."

"Thank you. I appreciate that."

"First, let's stop by the security office and get you your company ID and office key card. They're expecting us, so it shouldn't take too long."

Security processed my ID and key card in under fifteen minutes. Teresa led me up to the executive floor. As we stepped off the elevator I could see through the double glass doors into the CEO suite.

"That is Mr. Mitchell's office," Teresa said as she pointed out the suite in front of us. "Your office is just down the hall to the left," said Teresa as we turned and headed down the hallway.

Between her pointing things out to me, we were chatting, and I decided that I was going to like Teresa. She was warm, friendly, and capable.

"Pretty much everything you should need is on this floor. The executives and their staffs are all here. As your department and position are new, I can't speak to specifics. I do know that there are several workstations designated outside of your office for when you hire staff."

I was realizing that there was a lot I still didn't know about how my position and department was going to function day-to-day. Brandon had mentioned that he wanted me to build a team to meet the objectives that he laid out. I was hoping for a little more guidance once I settled in.

The hallway opened to a large room. A cluster of partitioned workstations were set up in the middle of the room. It looked pretty much like every other corporate office. I could hear voices of people talking on phones and the clack of computer keyboards.

Teresa led us past a series of empty workstations and stopped outside of an office. I could see through the open blinds that there was modern L-shaped desk and one of those ergonomic mesh chairs.

"Here we go. This is your office," said Teresa as she opened the door.

The office was little bigger than I thought it would be. Against the left wall was a file cabinet that matched the desk. Just beyond was a small table with two chairs. At the back of the office was a picture window with a nice view of the city.

"This is great," I said as I plopped my purse on top of the desk.

Teresa took the file folder she had been carrying and placed it on my desk.

"Here are all the employment forms that HR and Payroll need for you to fill out. If you let me know when you finish, I will pick them up and submit them for you. If you have any questions, just let me know."

"Thank you, Teresa. You've been very helpful."

"You're welcome. Here is my number," she said handing me her business card.

"All you need to do is dial my extension. If you need to make an outside call, hit 9 and then dial the number."

"Thanks," I said taking her card.

"Before I go, can I get you something to drink? We have coffee, tea, juice, and spring water."

"Oh, I don't want to bother you with that. If you show me where the coffee station is . . ."

"It's no bother at all. And I can give you a more thorough tour a little later."

"Well, alright then. I'd love a cup of coffee. One cream and one sugar, please."

"Okay. Be right back."

I settled into the chair behind my desk and opened the file folder. I pulled out the paperwork, grabbed a pen from the desk drawer and spent the next forty minutes completing the forms. The large coffee that Teresa brought me fueled my form-filling frenzy.

I called Teresa and told her that the forms were ready. After I hung up the phone it immediately rang. It caught me by surprise.

"Hello, Ashley Sullivan," I answered.

The voice on the other end introduced herself as Jacqueline Davenport's executive assistant. She asked if I had time to stop by Mrs. Davenport's office. I asked what time would be best. She stated Noon, and I told her I would be there then.

I checked my watch. It was 10:15. I wondered what I was going to do until then. Teresa knocked on my door. I waved her in.

"I'm here to pick up the forms, Ms. Sullivan."

"Yes. Thank you," I said handing her the folder. "Teresa, can you do me a favor?"

"Of course."

We planned out the rest of my morning with a tour, having IT set up my computer, and getting the basics set up in my office. At 11:55, Teresa showed me to Jacqueline Davenport's office.

"So, do you think I should be nervous that she wants to see me?" I asked as we headed down the hall.

"Oh, I wouldn't think so. I see her more than most because of being Mr. Mitchell's assistant. She is always nice. I know Mrs. Davenport's assistant well. She says the same."

"That's reassuring," I said.

We reached the elevator across from Brandon's office.

"Mrs. Davenport's office is through those doors," said Teresa.

"Thank you, Teresa."

"You're welcome, Ms. Sullivan."

"See you later," I said as Teresa stepped into Brandon's outer office.

I headed down the hall and into Mrs. Davenport's office suite.

Chapter 9

Mrs. Davenport's executive assistant greeted me as I entered. She looked to be in her mid-50's. She also looked like a former model. I wondered if everyone at the company was stunningly gorgeous.

"Hello, I'm Ashley Sullivan. Here to see Mrs. Davenport."

"Yes, of course. I'm Grace. Welcome to the company."

"Thank you."

"Let me tell her that you are here."

She picked up her phone. "Mrs. Davenport, Ms. Sullivan is here to see you." She waited for a response. "Yes, ma'am," she replied and hung up the phone.

"Let me show you in," said Grace as she got up from her desk.

Jacqueline Davenport was already standing and ready to greet me when Grace opened the door.

"Ashley, dear, please come in," said Mrs. Davenport.

Jacqueline Davenport was a tall, slender woman in her mid-70s. She looked at least ten years younger than that. I knew she started her career as a model and you could tell. She was still beautiful. She had a warm smile.

"It is nice to meet you, Mrs. Davenport," I said as we shook hands. Her hands were soft. Her touch was warm and welcoming.

"Please sit down," she said motioning to one of the chairs.

Mrs. Davenport's office had a modern glass and white trimmed desk with matching tables. She had comfortable matching white leather chairs. Fresh-cut flowers filled several crystal vases. Colorful modern art adorned the walls. Mrs. Davenport's credenza was covered with family photos.

She noticed that I was looking toward the photos. She went over and picked up one of the frames and handed it to me.

"This is Brandon when he was ten years old. That boy was a handful," she said with a chuckle. "Still is, in some ways."

"He was such a cute little boy," I said looking at the picture. His dark wavy hair and gorgeous blue eyes were unmistakable.

"That he was."

I placed the photo frame on the table. Mrs. Davenport sat in the chair opposite me.

"And you are such a lovely young woman."

I blushed. I was also a bit nervous. I had no idea about the direction of the conversation.

"Thank you."

"I know you are probably wondering why I invited you to visit with me today," she said.

I had no idea how best to respond.

"No need to answer, dear. I do want to assure you that I am not some senile old woman. There is a purpose for our meeting. Nothing, of course, that you should be nervous about."

"Yes, ma'am," I said.

"I wanted to meet you and welcome you to Jacqueline and Davenport Media."

"Thank you. I am delighted to be here. Working at Jacqueline has always been a dream of mine."

"Well, we are glad to have you as part of the Jacqueline family," she said patting my knee.

I was no longer nervous. I did have a feeling that there was more to our meeting than welcoming me to the company.

"I understand that you graduated from Davenport School of the Arts at Santa Barbara University. I also understand that you had an impressive record of academic achievement. And your application portfolio was stellar."

"Thank you, ma'am."

"Your new position has been in the works for some time. Brandon was searching for just the right person for the job. I'm confident he made the right decision in hiring you. I rarely question his business judgment. In that area, he has always displayed talent beyond his years."

I nodded. I didn't feel there was anything for me to add to the conversation at that point.

"With women, however, Brandon has shown less focus and commitment."

I couldn't believe she just threw that out there. She showed no signs of stopping either.

"He has dated many young women. And a few who were closer to his mother's age. All beautiful, of course. Brandon has an attraction to beautiful women like a moth to a flame. Can I be honest with you, dear?"

I thought she already had been. I was now curious to see what she considered an honest comment.

"Of course, Mrs. Davenport."

"Brandon hiring you has many layers. From a business perspective, we must have a top notch digital and social media presence. It is also important that the world see Brandon as more than an eligible bachelor unwilling to settle down. No small task for you, dear. I hope I am not scaring you."

"No, ma'am. I'm fine."

"Good. Is it okay if I get personal for a moment?"

"Yes, of course."

"I understand that Brandon has a personal interest in you. That he has taken you out a few times."

"Yes, ma'am. Brandon assured me that he would keep our personal and professional lives separate."

"Oh, dear, I'm not concerned about that. What I wanted to tell you is that I am glad that Brandon has taken an interest in you. You are a smart and attractive young woman."

"Thank you."

"Brandon is almost 30, it is time he starts taking a more serious interest in his romantic relationships. Don't get me wrong, I'm not trying to place any expectations or pressure on you."

"No, ma'am. I understand."

"Just know that I am pleased you are here. Brandon's decision to hire you may have been as personal as it was professional. For the first time I think his personal sense is as good as his business sense," she said as she placed her hand on top of mine.

Mrs. Davenport's phone buzzed and then Grace's voice came through the speaker.

"Mrs. Davenport, Mr. Mitchell just phoned and wanted you to know that he is back and on his way down."

"Thank you, Grace," Mrs. Davenport said loud enough to reach the speaker. She then turned back toward me.

"Well, speak of the devil." She stood, and I followed.

"I'm sure he was calling for your benefit and not mine," she said to me. "Enjoy the rest of your first day. I'm sure I'll see you soon."

"Thank you, Mrs. Davenport. It was such a pleasure to meet you."

"Oh, you are kind. The pleasure has been all mine."

There was a knock at the door and then Brandon walked in.

"Good afternoon, ladies," he said.

I couldn't imagine that I would ever get tired of seeing him walk into a room. He was gorgeous. He was wearing a stylish designer suit that formed to his frame. He looked every bit like he popped off the cover of GQ magazine.

"Hello, sweetie," said Mrs. Davenport as she gave Brandon a hug.

"Hello, grandmother."

"Did your morning go well?" Brandon asked me.

"Yes. I think I'm starting to get settled in."

"Great. Well, I just wanted to stop in and say hi. I have a late lunch meeting across town. May I steal Ashley to walk me out?"

"Oh yes. We're finished," said Mrs. Davenport.

"Thank you again, Mrs. Davenport," I said as Brandon and I turned to leave.

"Thank you for coming by."

We said goodbye to Grace in the outer office and pushed through the glass doors. Brandon pulled me around the corner. He wrapped his arms around me and kissed me.

"I thought of you all last night," he said.

"Really? I thought of you, too."

Brandon and I gazed into each other eyes. His sparkled like the Sun glistening off the Caribbean Ocean.

"Well, I need to run. Are you looking forward to Tavern on the Green this evening?"

"Very much," I replied. "It is a lovely day."

"Indeed. Perfect for an evening in Central Park. Have a great afternoon. See you at six."

With that Brandon turned and headed out for his lunch meeting. I wondered if Brandon's schedule was this full every day. I imagined it must be running such a large and high-profile company as Davenport Media.

I still couldn't believe I was now working and living in Manhattan and would be dining at Tavern on the Green and taking a horse-drawn carriage ride through Central Park. Somebody pinch me.

Chapter 10

Tavern on the Green was such an iconic restaurant. I had seen it in movies. I was happy to be taking in the experience in person.

It was a warm spring evening, so we sat at a table on the patio. Between the greenery on the patio and being at the edge of Central Park, it was easy to forget that we were in the center of Manhattan.

We decided to go a little more casual for dinner. Brandon was wearing charcoal gray dress slacks, a light blue dress shirt, unbuttoned at the collar, and a navy blue blazer. I had on a black skirt and a light pink blouse.

"So, what did you think about your fist day at work?" asked Brandon after we ordered.

"Well, I don't know if you can call getting my ID and filling out employment forms 'work'," I said.

"Necessary red tape. It will get more interesting. You have a lot on your plate getting the department up and running."

"Yes. I think I became more aware of that today. I'm hoping to gain some clarity on that from the CEO."

"Hmm. I suppose he can squeeze you in sometime this week."

"I'm serious, Brandon. I at least need to know some parameters around a budget, the hiring process, priorities..."

"I know. The learning curve is steep."

"You could say that."

"I'll have Teresa clear a block of time tomorrow and we can flesh out a plan."

"Thank you. She seems nice. Competent."

"You're welcome. Yes, she is. And, no, I've never dated her."

"I didn't ask about that."

"But you were thinking it."

"Maybe. Maybe not. I'll never tell."

Brandon just shrugged his shoulders and took a sip of his wine.

"My conversation with your grandmother was pretty interesting," I said as I buttered a dinner role.

"I was a little curious about that. I thought she might take a special interest in you."

"She approves of your hiring me. She also seems happy that we are dating."

"I figured she would be. My grandmother is pretty open minded. She also speaks her mind."

"Yes, she does."

"Oh no. What did she say?" Brandon asked with a blend of amusement and slight concern.

"Nothing much." I smiled at him and took a sip of wine.

"Ashley...don't be a tease."

"Just girl talk."

"Come on. What did she say?'

"Alright. It is not particularly attractive to see you beg."

Brandon just looked at me. He was waiting. I'd had my fun. I decided not to string him along any longer.

"She happened to mention, in her opinion, that you haven't paid the proper attention to your relationships with women."

Brandon just shook his head and laughed.

"Why does that not surprise me? She offer any other opinions?"

"Well, she believes you make good business decisions. In the case of hiring me, she said both your personal and business decisions were excellent."

"Did she now?"

"Well, I don't think she used the word 'excellent,' but that was the gist of it."

"Can't argue with her there," he said raising his wine glass. "To an excellent decision."

We touched glasses and laughed. It had been such a short time, but being with Brandon was easy. Easy on the eyes. Easy conversation. Easy everything.

I sat across from Brandon with a goofy grin on my face, still a bit dazzled that I was working for and dating one of the most handsome men on the planet. Was it possible that he would remain content with a regular girl like me?

Our dinner arrived, and we enjoyed a wonderful meal. I expressed how much I enjoyed the food and ambiance. Brandon promised that we would eat there again. We strolled into Central Park arm-in-arm for our romantic horse and carriage ride.

The evening air had turned cooler. I was glad. We cuddled under a light blanket as we rode the horse-drawn carriage through the park.

Central Park was an oasis in the middle of the bustling city. Riding along the winding trails of the park was like a fairy tale. Brandon and I shared a tender kiss and then I leaned in and nestled against his chest. It was a perfect romantic introduction to my new life in New York City.

Our forty-five-minute ride came to an end. I had enjoyed that time with Brandon under the stars and trees. Brandon tipped the driver and then assisted me out of the carriage. He took me by the hand.

"My place is a short walk from here," he said as we began strolling out of the park.

"Do you have a view of Central Park?" I asked.

"Yes. You can see over the top of the park and to the buildings surrounding it. A great view. Day or night. We have the walk signal, let's cross."

We crossed the street and approached the front door to his building. The doorman greeted us as he held open the door.

"Good evening, Mr. Mitchell. Good evening, Miss."

"Good evening, Thomas," said Brandon.

The lobby of his building was beautiful with a lot of marble.

"The main elevators go to every floor. The elevator at the end of the hall is private and express to the Penthouse," Brandon told me as he pulled out a key card to access his private elevator. I don't know why Brandon living in the penthouse surprised me. I guess a lot of this was still so new to me.

I was sure the penthouse was luxurious. I had no doubt that the view of Central Park was impressive. They say everything's bigger in Texas, but Brandon's world was proving to be incredible. It was now my world, too.

Chapter 11

It didn't take long to reach the Penthouse. The elevator doors opened into the living room. A wall of windows offered a sweeping view of Central Park and its surrounding buildings. A large terrace ran the full length of the Penthouse.

The inside was modern and almost minimalist. It was not empty or cold though. Warm art adorned the walls. There were also framed photos of Brandon with family and friends.

The leather furniture looked comfortable. Glass and polished metal tables were like the ones in his office. Mounted to the wall above the fireplace was a large plasma TV.

"That is great for watching Yankees games. Although, I prefer to go in person, when I can," he said as he took off his sport coat and draped it over the back of one of the living room chairs.

"Do you like baseball?" he asked.

"Sorry. Not really. My dad loves it though."

"Is he a Yankees fan? Wait. Maybe the Rangers or Astros?"

"Well, the Rangers are in Arlington, near Dallas. The Astros are in Houston. The Austin metro area is sort of in-between. So, I guess, either could be his team . . ."

"Sounds like you're trying to avoid answering the question, Ms. Sullivan," he said as he looped his arms around my waist.

"Um. . . my dad is from New England. Maine."

"A Red Sox fan?!" Brandon grabbed his chest. "Say it isn't so?!" he teased.

"Sorry. So. He'd say the same about you being a Yankees fan."

"Good thing I like you so much," he said as he kissed me on the cheek.

"I figure I'll avoid mentioning the Yankees to my dad just yet."

"Have you said anything to your family . . . about us?"

"Not yet. I will. It's just kinda soon to mention it to them. You have no idea how they can be. Especially my mom."

"No need to explain. How about a tour?"

"Yes, please."

Brandon showed me around the downstairs. Off the living room there was a gourmet chef's kitchen and a formal dining room. Down a hall was a study, a guest bedroom and bathroom, and a half-bath. A winding staircase led upstairs. Brandon showed me four large bedrooms, each with their own bathroom.

"I've saved the best for last," he said as he took me by the hand and led me down the long hallway. At the end of the hall were two large double doors. He opened them and led me into the master bedroom. His bedroom was quite large, complete with a furnished sitting area. Windows offered a similar view of Central Park as from the living room downstairs.

A large king-sized bed looked almost small in the room. The master bathroom was as nice as any five-star resort. Monogrammed towels, and a robe hung from hooks.

"So, what do you think?" Brandon asked.

"It's beautiful. But what do you do with all the space?"

"I entertain a lot. Out-of-town friends often stay over to take in New York. One day, I suppose, it will be enough room for a family."

"It's nice being right across from the park," I commented as I looked out the window.

"It is," I heard him say into my ear as he wrapped his arms around my waist. He brushed my hair to the side and kissed my neck. I felt a now familiar tingle. Familiar, but no less wonderful.

We stood on the patio and looked out over Central Park as the stars in the night sky twinkled like diamonds and a soft glow shimmered from the buildings surrounding the park. A gentle breeze swept upward and tossed my hair gently to one side.

I was happy to be in the moment with the most incredible man I had ever met. Brandon and I talked for hours before he had me select one of the guest rooms for me to stay in.

"Not the Four Seasons," he said, "but I think you should be comfortable. I'd like you to stay until the lease on your apartment starts next week."

"That is sweet of you, but I don't want to be an imposition."

Brandon opened his arms wide and moved in a sweeping motion. "Look around. I'm rattling around this place all by myself. It doesn't make any sense to have you staying at a hotel when I have plenty of room."

"What would people think if they knew I was staying over?"

"They can think whatever they want. It has all been said about me before." Brandon then paused a beat. "Unless it makes you uncomfortable. I guess I haven't stopped to think the spotlight is new to you."

I nodded, but wanted to put Brandon at ease. I really wasn't troubled by gossip. "No, it is okay. Besides, it is only for a few days. If anyone asks we will tell them the truth. It is always the best policy."

"Well, you are the social media specialist. Towels and toiletries are all laid out in the bathroom, along with a bathrobe."

"Better than a hotel," I said grinning.

"I had Thomas collect your luggage from the hotel," said Brandon as he pointed out my suitcases sitting in the corner.

"Thank you," I said. "What if I had declined your invitation to stay?"

"Then we would have booked you a hotel room and Thomas would lug the suitcases back."

"He's probably glad not to have moved my luggage a second time tonight."

"I'm sure he is." Brandon gave a kiss and then stepped toward the door. "Good night, Ashley."

I blew him a kiss as he closed the door behind him. I twirled around and fell back on the bed. As I stared up at the ceiling I couldn't help but break out in a wide smile as the joy bubbled up from inside of me.

Chapter 12

Three Months Later...

Summer passed and Labor Day was just around the corner. I had settled into my position, hired staff, and felt in control of the Digital and Social Media department. Chelsea arrived in New York mid-August and had completed orientation at Columbia Law School.

I had rented a nice two bedroom, two bath apartment off Central Park in early June. I waited until Chelsea moved in so we could shop for the finishing touches. I wanted her to feel at home in the apartment. Besides, shopping is always more fun with your BFF.

Brandon and I traveled a lot together for work. In New York we found a nice balance between being together and having time on our own.

I told my family that I was dating Brandon. I received the complete quizzing that I had expected. I told them that it was getting serious, but that was as much as they were going to get out of me.

A major setback was the news in July that my dad had lost his job of 30 years due to "downsizing." The Texas economy was doing well, but that didn't seem to help a mid-level manager in his 50s find a decent job. They had borrowed against the equity in their house to pay for my sister to start college in the fall. Not that there is ever a good time to lose your job, but the timing couldn't have been worse.

I was fortunate that I could financially help them out. My parents refused at first, but I insisted. I convinced them that it made no sense for them to lose their house, go without health insurance, or for my sister to drop out of college before she even started. It stretched my budget, but I would get by.

I had decided not to tell either Chelsea or Brandon about my family's situation. Chelsea would feel guilty about not paying rent. Brandon would feel compelled to help. I didn't want him to think I was asking. Nor did I want the stress of my family taking money from him.

The Friday of Labor Day weekend most of the office went home early. Brandon had been out of town a few days and would be back later that evening. We were leaving in the morning for a long weekend at his family's home in the Hamptons.

Chelsea had met a fellow law student,, and they had gone out a couple of times. She seemed to like him. She wanted to cook him a romantic dinner at our place. I told her that I would just go over to Brandon's for the night.

I packed for the weekend in the Hamptons and headed over to Brandon's. I decided Chelsea had a good idea. I would surprise Brandon with dinner at his place. I texted him I would be coming over for the evening, leaving out the surprise about dinner. He wouldn't see my message until after he landed. I was walking the four blocks between our apartments when I bumped into Thomas, Brandon's doorman.

"Hello, Ms. Sullivan," he said.

"Oh, hi, Thomas."

"I just got off work and I'm on my way to the subway. You heading to Mr. Mitchell's?"

"Yes. A little change in plans tonight. Thought I would surprise him."

"That's nice. I'm sure he'll be happy to see you step off the elevator."

"What? Is he already home?"

"Yes, ma'am. About a half-hour ago. Said he got home early from his business trip."

"Thank you, Thomas. Have a nice Labor Day weekend."

"Thank you, Ms. Sullivan. You have a nice weekend as well."

I continued on toward Brandon's building. I wondered why Brandon hadn't responded to my text message. I pulled out my phone and checked again. Nothing. Must be showering and changing.

I arrived at Brandon's building.

"Hello, Ms. Sullivan," said Anthony, the doorman who had the shift after Thomas.

"Hello, Anthony."

I pulled the Penthouse elevator key card out of my purse and swiped it to open the door. I stepped in and waited for the doors to close. The elevator reached the Penthouse,, and the doors opened. The lights in the living room were dim,, and the fireplace was on. How sweet. Brandon must have received my text and set a romantic mood for dinner.

I didn't even make it off the elevator. My jaw hit the floor. I had no words or breath. I felt like I had been punched in the stomach.

Standing in front of the fireplace was another woman with her arms around Brandon's neck. He immediately broke free of her. "Ashley! Wait!" he called out as he rushed toward the elevator. I had already hit the button to close the doors.

As I stood alone in the elevator and watched the doors shut, I fought back the tears that I knew were coming. I leaned against the back wall and grabbed the handrail as my hands shook and my legs began to buckle beneath me. The elevator descended to the lobby and I felt as if I was descending into my own personal pit of despair. The tears I fought so hard to hold back began streaming down my face. Shock and rage was now empty desolation.

I wiped my face with the back of my hands in an attempt to regain composure, but my head was spinning. Once breathless from sensual pleasure, I found myself gasping for air from a pit of darkness and pain. Joy and wonder at all the promise our relationship offered had been replaced with a void of utter despair. Only by getting as far away as possible could I begin to find release from the suffering and heartache.

I had let myself believe I was in some sort of romantic fairy tale, but my fairy tale had turned into a nightmare. I had been taken in by Brandon's charms . . . only to be tossed aside like all the others. Maybe what we had had never been real . . . just a lie all along.

What was I going to do now? How could he explain what I saw? He couldn't. It was over between us.

What about my job? Our personal and professional lives were suppose to be separate. But I didn't see how I could continue to work for him. My family! Oh, no! They need me to keep my job.

I couldn't think about it now. I was crying harder. My head was throbbing. I hit the stop button. I sank to the floor of the elevator and buried my face into my hands. I let the tears flow. How could he do this to me?

I reached the lobby and the doors opened. I stepped out of the elevator pulling my luggage behind me. I crossed the lobby toward the front door.

"Everything okay, Ms. Sullivan?" asked Anthony.

"Ashley! Please wait!" Brandon pleaded behind me.

I turned as he stepped off one of the main elevators into the lobby.

"Ashley, we need to talk." Standing there, crushed, I had to decide what to do next.

Chapter 13

It had been less than five minutes since I saw Brandon in the arms of another woman. In an instant, he crushed my spirit. Now we were facing each other in the lobby of his building.

He came after me. Did that count for something? Could he explain his compromising position? I was still reeling and unable to process much of anything.

"Anthony, please give us a moment," Brandon said to the doorman.

"That okay, Ms. Sullivan?" Anthony still looked concerned about the situation.

"Yes. Thank you, Anthony. I'll be okay."

I doubted that I would be okay. But I knew I was safe. Brandon may have cheated, but he wouldn't harm me.

"I'll be right outside the door," Anthony said as he pushed through the front door.

"Ashley, please give me a chance to explain," Brandon said.

"Explain what?! Explain the woman in your arms? The romantic mood lighting? The roaring fire in the fireplace?!"

"Ashley, nothing happened."

"Yet. Tonight. Am I supposed to believe that nothing was going to happen? That nothing has happened since we started dating?"

Brandon looked down and stood in silence.

"Brandon, answer me!"

"I promise nothing was going to happen tonight. I can explain what you saw..."

I had regained some presence of mind. I needed Brandon to be honest with me. No matter how much it might hurt me further, no matter the cost. I needed the truth. He owed me that.

"Tonight. You can promise nothing was going to happen tonight. What you didn't say is that nothing has happened before tonight. Have you cheated on me or not?"

"Ashley, it's not that simple..."

"Yes, it is that simple. Have you cheated on me? 'Yes' or 'no'?"

"Ashley, I don't ever want to hurt you. Let's sit down and talk."

"Answer the question!"

"I'm sorry . . . technically, yes . . . I've cheated. But, Ashley..."

"No. Don't say another word to me," I said as I fought through a new round of tears.

"It's over between us." I turned and Anthony opened the door for me and I exited the building.

"Can I get you a cab, Ms. Sullivan?" Asked Anthony.

"No, thank you, Anthony."

I started walking toward my apartment, but without a real sense of direction. I just ended a relationship with the man of my dreams. Or I so I had led to believe. A man who I had fallen for. I thought Brandon, and I were building a long-term relationship. Now, I was heartbroken, angry, and alone.

"Hey, baby. You're lookin' fine tonight. Where you headin'?" Some creep called out to me.

"Get lost!" I retorted as I walked past him. He made me nervous, but he didn't want to mess with me. I had so much rage inside that he would regret any further move toward me.

He took the hint and continued in the other direction.

I walked the remaining blocks to my building. As I waited for the elevator I remembered that Chelsea was having dinner with her date in the apartment. Darn! I thought.

I didn't want to disturb them. At the same time I wanted to take a hot shower and go to bed. It's a big enough apartment. I'll go straight to my bedroom.

The elevator dinged, and the doors opened. I flashed back to the doors opening to Brandon's penthouse.

"Jerk!" I said aloud as I stepped into the elevator. I wiped my face as best I could on the elevator ride up. I gained as much composure as possible.

I took deep breath as I reached my door. I fumbled for my key as my hand shook. I managed to unlock the door. Chelsea and her date were at the dining room table.

"Oh, hey, Ash. Did you forget something?" Asked Chelsea.

"No. Change in plans. Don't let me interrupt you guys. I'm just going to my room."

Chelsea knew something was wrong. She also didn't want to be rude and not introduce me to her date.

"Ashley, this is Wes Griffin. Wes, this is Ashley Sullivan."

"Pleased to meet you," said Wes as he shook my hand.

"Nice to meet you, Wes."

"Is everything okay?" asked Chelsea.

"Everything is fine. I'm just not feeling well. I'm going to take a hot shower and turn in for the evening."

I faked the best smile I could muster.

"Enjoy your evening," I said.

"I hope you feel better," said Wes.

"Thank you. I'll be fine. 'Night guys."

I padded down the hall to my bedroom. No sooner had I closed my bedroom door then I heard a short knock and Chelsea entered.

"Okay, liar. What is going on?" She closed the door behind her.

I didn't want to ruin her evening. I figured we could talk tomorrow. I just wanted to crawl under the covers and hide from the world for a while.

"Chels, I'm just not feeling well. That's all."

"Not true. This is me you're talking to, remember?"

"Can we talk about this tomorrow? You have a date over. He is cute, by the way."

"No way. You are not changing the subject," Chelsea said crossing her arms.

I knew better than to expect Chelsea to let it go without some explanation.

"If I tell you, you have to promise to let it go until tomorrow. That you will go back and enjoy your date."

"Depends on what it is."

"No conditions. Promise. I mean it."

"Okay. I promise."

"I broke up with Brandon."

"What?! Ashley, what happened?"

"Nope. You promised. Now that you know, you need to go back to your date. It can wait until tomorrow."

"No it can't," said Chelsea.

"Chelsea, I just want to take a hot shower and curl up under the covers. Forget the world for a while."

"Nope. I'm breaking my promise. I'll explain to Wes. He will understand."

"You will do no such thing Chelsea Richards. There is no point in my ruining your evening."

"Right. Like I am going to go off and enjoy a date when my best friend just broke up with her boyfriend."

"I'll be fine," I protested.

Chelsea ignored my protest.

"Just give me a few minutes to explain to Wes. Then I'll be back and we can talk."

I didn't bother to argue. Chelsea had made up her mind and there would be no talking her out of her decision. I had to admit that talking with Chelsea was better than crying myself to sleep.

"Okay. Thanks. I'm going to take a quick shower."

I was a mess and needed the shower. *How could you do this to me? Wasn't I good enough for you?* I thought. I knew that I shouldn't blame myself. It wasn't my fault.

"Don't do it to yourself, Ashley," I heard Chelsea's voice from behind me.

I turned and faced her as she stood in my doorway.

"Don't do what?"

"Beat yourself up over this. Second guess what you should have done differently. It's not your fault."

It was amazing how well Chelsea knew me. Sometimes I wondered if she understood me better than I understood myself. At the same time, I had lingering doubt. I felt that I held back my sexual exploration with Brandon.

"Brandon's an idiot," Chelsea offered.

I couldn't help it. I burst into tears. Chelsea pulled me tight and hugged me.

"I'm sorry, sweetie," she said.

"He cheated on me Chels," I sobbed. "I can't believe he was seeing another women at the same time he was dating me."

"He's scum. He doesn't deserve you."

"That's what hurts the most," I said as I pulled back and wiped my face, "I don't think he is scum, Chels. I saw something more in him. There is something deeper. More emotional and intimate."

"It must not run very deep," Chelsea said with an edge in her voice.

She was upset with Brandon for hurting me. I knew she wouldn't want to hear anything good about him. She wanted less for me to say anything good about him.

"I broke up with him. I ended it because he cheated. Despite that – "

"No. No. No. Don't even think it, Ashley."

"Chelsea, you know me. You know I can't let go so easily."

"Exactly my point. I know you can't let go easily. But it is what you need to do."

"It's to final," I sighed.

"Ashley, I love you. You're the sister I never had. That's why it makes me crazy to hear you talk like this."

"He cheated. He broke my heart. I don't know if I can ever get over that. But I had an undeniable attraction to him. I don't know if I can ever get over that either."

"Ashley, right now he doesn't deserve that type of consideration. He was seeing another woman. At least the one we know of. He doesn't get a free pass for that. Not now. Not ever."

"I know. I was clear with him. I told him that it was over."

"Now you just need to convince yourself of that," said Chelsea.

I was emotionally and physically exhausted. Chelsea was trying to give me some of her steel resolve. I wasn't there yet.

"I'm going to take my shower now. Maybe that will help me feel better," I said.

"Good idea. There's a new carton of ice cream in the freezer. I'll meet you at the kitchen table with two spoons," replied Chelsea.

I nodded my approval. I went into my bathroom and closed the door. I undressed and stepped into the shower. I let the hot water wash over me and loosen my tense muscles.

After my shower I put on a pair of pajamas and joined Chelsea at the kitchen table.

"What flavor?" I asked.

"Chocolate Chip Cookie Dough," answered Chelsea.

"Great. Hand me a spoon."

"A first step in moving on," said Chelsea as she dug her spoon into the ice cream.

I followed her lead. Ice cream wouldn't fix everything, but it wouldn't hurt either.

My emotions were still raw. I knew that it would take time for the hurt and anger to go away. I also knew that Chelsea was right. I had no choice but to move on with my life.

Chapter 14

I had a restless night, but managed to get a few hours of sleep. When I woke I noticed that I had a text message from Brandon.

Brandon: Ashley, No words can express how sorry I am. Please give me a chance to explain...to make it up to you. Let's get away. We can go to the Hamptons like we planned. We can go anywhere you want. Just please call.

I was tempted to call. Then I thought better of it. I was afraid he would talk me into getting back together with him. I needed more time.

Chelsea knocked on my door.

"You up?" she called through the door.

"Come on in," I answered.

I held up my phone. "Text from Brandon," I said.

"What did he say?" Chelsea asked.

I handed her my phone. She read his message.

"Tell him to get lost," she said as she handed my phone back to me.

"Should I even respond?"

"No. You told him it was over. It's over. If I were you I'd delete him from your contacts and block his number."

"I'm not sure..."

"I know you won't do that. I'm just saying what I would do. For now, at least, don't respond. Maybe he will get the hint."

"Thanks for being here for me last night," I said.

"No problem . . . Listen, I was thinking that you need a fun night out. No moping around allowed this weekend. And, before you say 'no', hear me out."

"Okay," I said.

"Wes and I want to check out a new restaurant. A group of our friends from school are going tonight. We want you to come with us."

"I don't feel like going out."

"Come on, Ash. You need to get out of the apartment. Let loose. Have some fun," Chelsea pleaded.

I wasn't feeling particularly social at the moment. On the other hand, I didn't want to spend the entire holiday weekend feeling sorry for myself.

"I can see your wheels spinning," said Chelsea. "Does that mean you are re-considering?"

"I'll think about it. Talk to me later," I said.

Chelsea worked on convincing me all day. I relented and agreed to go for a couple of drinks. I made no promises beyond that. Chelsea took the small victory.

Thanks to my salary and expense account, I had a closet full of nice outfits. Everything from casual to professional. From cute dresses to stunning gowns. I had no excuse. Chelsea wasn't going to let me off the hook.

I decided on a teal bloused chiffon bodice. It had a scoop neckline with long sleeves and elasticized wrist cuffs. I paired it with an Aztec sequin skirt.

I had avoided crying all day. I couldn't hold back the tears any longer. I sat on my bed and sobbed, soaking up handfuls of tissue from the bathroom in minutes.

"Whoa, whoa, whoa," Chelsea said bursting into my bedroom. "None of that tonight."

She sat next to me and put her arm around my shoulders. She pulled me toward her and patted my arm.

"Ash, I know it still hurts. It will for a while. But it will hurt less each day."

I wiped my eyes and blew my nose.

"I know," I said. "I just had a moment, that's all."

"You're allowed. But we are going to have a great time tonight. Help you forget a bit."

"Not sure that is what I'm looking for tonight."

"Sweetie, you won't have to look. I think it is going to find you. Just be ready to take it."

"We'll see," I said as I headed into the bathroom to freshen up.

Wes arrived a few minutes later, and we left for the club. Wes must have been good luck as we hailed a cab right away. He gave the driver the address, and we settled in for Saturday evening traffic.

"I'm glad that you decided to join us," Wes said to me.

"Thanks. Although, I'm not sure I had much of a choice. Your date is pretty tenacious."

"You should see her in mock trial class. She's like a pit bull," Wes said as he patted Chelsea on the knee.

"Doesn't surprise me in the least," I said.

"Okay. Enough talking about me," Chelsea said.

Wes seemed like a nice guy. It was easy to see why Chelsea liked him. He was good looking, smart, and easy-going. I was betting that he was a good match for her.

When we arrived at the club, there was a long line out the door.

"Do you think we'll get in?" I asked.

"Yep. We are on the VIP list," answered Chelsea.

"How did we manage that?" I said.

"My roommate is a waiter at the restaurant. He scored us the VIP table," said Wes.

"Cute and connected," said Chelsea as she hugged his arm.

Wes gave our names to the host, and he showed us toward our table.

"There they are," said Wes as he nodded toward a group of people sitting at a table near the back. One of the girls was motioning for us to come over. We made our way through the restaurant to the back table.

Wes and Chelsea introduced me to their law school friends. I learned that one of the guys, Rick, was from Austin and had attended the University of Texas. I told him that I knew several high school classmates who had attended UT. He remarked that his best friend from UT was visiting New York for the weekend. He would be back in a moment from getting a drink.

"Ashley. Ashley Sullivan." I heard a familiar voice behind me.

I turned and saw Jeremy Wagner. A guy that I briefly dated in high school. There are over eight million people living in New York City, plus visitors. I figured that the odds were pretty low, nearly non-existent, that I would randomly bump into someone I knew from high school back in Texas.

"You two know each other?" asked Rick.

"Yes. We went to high school together," said Jeremy.

"We actually dated for a while," I added. I'm not sure why I volunteered that piece of information.

"Wow. Small world," commented Rick.

"So, you are Rick's friend from the University of Texas," I said to Jeremy.

"Yep. I'm visiting for the long weekend."

"My parents had mentioned that you moved to Manhattan," Jeremy told me. "I never thought I would bump into you."

I can't say that I was disappointed at the chance meeting. I had always been fond of Jeremy. A nice guy and very cute. He had been a good boyfriend.

"Yes. I'm the new Director of Digital and Social Media at Jacqueline magazine."

"Sounds fancy. Good for you. I always knew you would end up with a great job."

"Thanks. What are you doing?" I asked Jeremy with genuine interest.

"I just moved to Los Angeles. I'm in the marketing department at Pacific Coast Pictures."

"Wow. The movie studio? That must be exciting."

"Well, it's not like I'm meeting movie stars or anything like that. But I love what I do. It is fun promoting the movies."

Jeremy and I ordered more drinks and got caught up. I introduced him to Chelsea and Wes. I hated to admit it, but I was having a nice time. Nice music began from an orchestra and couples moved onto a small dance floor. I felt like we were at a wedding reception.

"Would you like to dance?" Jeremy asked.

I paused a beat before answering. "Sure," I then said.

Jeremy extended his hand, and I took it. We walked to the dance floor and began to sway to the music. It was an instrumental version of a popular song. Chelsea and Wes joined next to us on the dance floor.

"This takes me back to school dances in the gym," Jeremy said.

"The music and atmosphere are a bit different."

"True. A fancy New York establishment is nothing compared to a bunch of sweaty teenagers breathing in the stale air of a high school gymnasium in central Texas."

We both laughed. I had forgotten what an easy-going and pleasant guy Jeremy had been in high school. He hadn't seemed to change in the past four years.

Brandon flashed into my mind. I pulled away from Jeremy. He looked both surprised and disappointed.

"I'm sorry," I said.

"Is something wrong?" Jeremy asked.

"No. Yes. No . . . I don't know," I stammered.

"Give us a sec," said Chelsea to Jeremy as she pulled me aside.

"Ash, what is wrong with you? You were having a good time. Don't over think this."

"I was. But...but, then I thought of Brandon. Chels, maybe I'm just not ready." I said.

"Forget Brandon. You don't owe him a thing!"

Chelsea paused for a moment to let what she said sink in. Not that I needed a reminder. Or maybe I did. Maybe I needed to be reminded that I did nothing wrong and was free to do as I pleased without guilt.

"Let me ask you this. . .do you like Jeremy?" asked Chelsea.

"I did. In high school. I told you we dated."

"Not what I meant. Do you like him enough to enjoy the evening with him?"

I thought for a moment. My head was swirling. I was also conflicted.

"I guess you are right," I proclaimed.

I walked over to Jeremy.

"I just broke up with my boyfriend. You live in LA and I live here. I'm not looking for a date, but it would be nice to continue dancing with you and catching up on old times."

Jeremy nodded in an understanding nod. "Sure. I'd like that very much."

We danced, enjoyed a pleasant dinner, and then went for ice cream. Jeremy shared what it was like living in Hollywood and we caught up on what was going on with each of our families. He had already heard about my dad losing his job, but no one knew I was supporting my family. Everyone assumed my dad had more of a severance package than he had actually received.

"It was nice seeing you again," I said to Jeremy as he walked me to the front door of my building.

"Great seeing you again, Ashley." He shook his head.

"What?" I asked.

"I don't know how I ever let you get away."

"I went to college in California."

"Do you ever wonder where things would be now if we had stayed together?"

I didn't want to hurt Jeremy's feelings, but I hadn't given it any thought. He had been nice high school boyfriend, but all I ever wanted to do was be in the fashion business in New York or Paris.

"Oh, I don't know, Jeremy. What we had in high school was very nice. But I wasn't ready for anything serious back then."

"And now?" Jeremy asked. Where was he going with this?

"I'm flattered, but you live in Hollywood and I am here in New York. Besides, are we even the same people?"

"It has only been four years. I'm still the same person. I always will be. I think you are pretty much the same, too. Just smarter and prettier."

I easily blushed at most compliments. This time was no different. "You're sweet to say that."

I think Jeremy could tell from my body language this wasn't going anywhere. "Well, I should get back to Wes," he said after a few awkward beats of silence. "I don't want to end up on the street tonight."

"Maybe if circumstances were different," I offered as a balm. "Maybe if we didn't live on different coasts . . . if I hadn't just broken up with my boyfriend."

"I guess timing is everything in life."

"I guess." I then paused a beat. Jeremy had nothing more to say.

"Thanks for the ice cream," I said after another beat. "It really was wonderful catching up with you." There . . . polite, friendly, and completely void of anything even hinting at rekindling any high school romance.

"Good night, Ashely." Jeremy offered an awkward hug.

"Good night, Jeremy. Keep in touch and say hi to your family for me."

Jeremy nodded and offered a faint smile. I pushed through the door and into the lobby of my apartment building. While Jeremy wasn't the guy for me, it had been nice to see him and help take my mind off of Brandon. I only hoped these were the first steps in letting go and moving on.

Chapter 15

I woke early after a somewhat restless night of sleep. I had slept better than the night before, but still not my usual night's rest. I went to the bathroom to check my look in the mirror. Not that bad, I thought as I checked for puffiness under my eyes. A little makeup and I'd be okay.

I knew I couldn't get away with it for long though. I would have to start sleeping better. Baggy eyes and zombie-walking through the day was not far behind if I didn't get my requested amount of beauty rest.

I decided to check if Chelsea was back from her morning run as we had made plans for Sunday brunch at a little cafe around the corner from our apartment. I walked through the apartment and I was still alone. I didn't think she'd be back this early, but I was already a little hungry and hoped we could catch brunch on the earlier side.

I put on a pot of coffee and then headed back toward my room to shower and get dressed. My cell phone was vibrating as I walked into my bedroom. I picked it up from my bedside table. It was Brandon.

I thought about whether I should answer. At some point I needed to make it clear that I intended on keeping my job. In the beginning we had agreed to keep our personal and professional lives as separate as possible. Friday night I wasn't sure if that was possible. After some thought on Saturday, I realized that we had to stick to the agreement.

By all accounts I was doing a great job. I loved the working world I found myself in and the salary was phenomenal. I also didn't have much of an option. I needed to keep that salary.

My dad was getting interviews, but my family still needed my financial help. I was the only thing standing in the way of them losing their house, insurance, and my sister not being able to attend college. Leaving my job at Jacqueline was not an option.

I stared at Brandon's name on my phone. I had removed his picture. That made it a little easier.

Despite Chelsea's urging, I couldn't just delete him off my phone. Or out of my life. Not completely. I did still work for him.

I waited until the third ring. One more and he'll go to voicemail I decided that was my best play. Let him either leave a message or hang up. I needed more time.

More time to decide exactly what I wanted to say to him. I knew that I wanted to go short and sweet. Well, short anyway. I hadn't decided on sweet yet.

He cheated, he still had a hold on me. I had cared for him deeply. I couldn't just shut that off completely. Not in a little more than a day.

How long would it take? One month? Two months? Longer? Every day it would probably get easier to let go and move on.

My voice mail dinged with a new message. Okay, he decided to leave a message. Not now. I put my phone down and headed to the bathroom. I stopped. I went back and picked up the phone.

I hit the message to listen: "Ashley, I can't say sorry enough times. For the rest of my life . . ." I hit the stop button and put the phone back down. No. I'm not ready yet. I looked at the phone sitting on my table. Nope. Taking my shower.

I went into the bathroom and started the water. A hot shower always felt so good. The bathroom was like a steam room by the time I finished. Turning off the water, I stepped out of the shower, grabbed a towel and began drying myself off.

Standing there, I couldn't help but wonder if this was how it was going to be or if I was just overreacting. I could hear my mother's voice inside my head saying, "Ashley, don't get so hysterical." Admitting that I could have that tendency was of little consolation.

After I dressed, I picked up my phone and listened to the rest of Brandon's message. I played it back two more times. I took a deep breath and touched 'dial' on my screen. I anxiously waited as the phone rang.

My heart raced faster as Brandon answered.

Chapter 16

"Ashley, I'm glad you called . . ."

"Brandon, wait," I interjected. I had worked up my nerve to call him back. I needed to say what I needed to say and get off the phone. My episode in the shower proved to me that I still ached for Brandon.

Maybe what I needed was more time. Maybe we needed more time to arrive at a place where we could work something out. I wanted to be firm in not giving in to my desire for him. At the same time, I needed to leave the door open to the possibility of reconciliation

"This isn't going to be a conversation," I continued. "I need you to know that my calling doesn't change anything right now."

"Ashley can we . . ."

"I'm not finished. When I say what I need to say I am hanging up. Understood?" I said.

"Yes," he replied. Brandon was not used to being in the position he found himself in. I think, however, he realized he had no choice but to accept my terms of the phone call. It was the first response he had received from me since I left him Friday night.

I took a quick breath to steady my voice. Then I continued.

"I expect you to honor our agreement that our personal relationship and professional relationship were separate. I have no intention of leaving my job at Jacqueline. Unless you have a good reason to fire me, I will be in the office Tuesday morning. Unless I say otherwise, please refrain from contacting me for anything other than business. That is all I wanted to tell you. I'm hanging up." I hit 'end call' and put my phone down.

I sat on my bed and took a deep breath. My hands were shaking. But I had done it. I said what I need to say to him. My text message tone chirped.

I glanced down at the screen.

Brandon: Meet me in my office Tue 8:30 am. Brief business matter to discuss.

"He has got to be kidding." I said aloud. I figured I didn't have a reason to say no.

Me: Fine. See you Tue 8:30 am.

I didn't believe for one second that it was just a business matter. I only hoped that I could keep my longing for him in check. It would be easy to give in to temptation. I hated that I knew that to be true.

"Ashley, you home?" I heard Chelsea call from the living room.

"Be right there," I answered. I put my phone down and headed to the living room.

Chelsea stood in her running clothes and drank a bottle of water.

"So, how did things go with Jeremy?" she asked. I didn't bother to wait up for Chelsea to get home last night. I just wanted to go to bed and try not to think about Brandon.

"It was okay," I said. "Want some coffee?"

"What? That's all you going to tell me?"

"There is really nothing to tell. I'm really hungry. Can we leave for brunch?"

"Let me shower and change, then we can go. But I know there must be more to your story. You can tell me at brunch."

I was able to finish my cup of coffee while Chelsea got ready. She actually made record time showering and getting dressed. I knew she was anxious to hear about my night with Jeremy. I had been trying to decide how to approach the conversation. Chelsea was going to flip out over the fact that Brandon still consumed so many of my thoughts.

I needed to be selective. Lead with my phone call to Brandon. Only mention how firm I was with him. I hoped she wouldn't probe any further. I also knew better than that.

"Okay, ready to go," Chelsea announced as she returned to the living room.

Chelsea tried to pry details out of me as we walked the half block to the cafe. I would have no part of it and kept her waiting. I diverted the conversation to her night with Wes. She was champing at the bit to hear about my night, but settled for telling me about hers until after we placed our order with the waiter.

It pleased me that Chelsea liked Wes. She was clearly happy with him and it seemed they were setting the foundation for a serious relationship. Chelsea deserved a loving partner.

For as many guys as Chelsea had dated, she hadn't met that special someone. Maybe Wes would turn out to be the right guy for her. I hoped so.

"Okay, Ash. We've ordered. Spill the beans," she said the second the waiter had left our table.

I had never lied to Chelsea. I never would. But I reminded myself that I needed to frame what I said carefully. She could read me like a book. I didn't want all my chapters read over brunch.

"I'm starting with this morning and working backwards. However, there is a method to my madness," I started.

"Bummer. I hope your story is going to be interesting," said Chelsea as she poured cream into her coffee.

"Will you let me tell it my way, please," I said passing her a packet of Stevia that I knew she would ask for in about two seconds.

"Thanks," she said acknowledging the packet of sweetener.

"You're welcome. Now, promise me you will not interrupt," I said.

"I promise," said Chelsea raising her right hand.

"Good. I spoke with Brandon . . ."

"What?!" Chelsea interjected.

"What part of not interrupting do you need explained to you," I retorted.

Chelsea held up her hands in surrender.

"He called and left me a message. Very apologetic. He seemed sincere in wanting to own what he did," I explained.

I could tell from Chelsea's body language that she did not like the words that had come out of my mouth.

"Relax, Chels. I called him back . . ."

I thought Chelsea was going to reach over the table and strangle me. At some point we would probably need to address her level in trust for how I handle situations. I ignored her flaring nostrils and continued to tell her what I had said to Brandon on the phone. She seemed satisfied.

"Ash, I'm sorry. I was so caught up in how what he did impacted you personally, I didn't even think about what that could have meant for your career."

"That's okay, Chels. I only really considered it yesterday. I'm good with the decision I made. I'll need to see how it plays out," I replied.

So far Chelsea didn't seem to have any follow-up questions. If that continued, I could probably avoid discussing my continued longing for Brandon. I wasn't ready for that conversation with Chelsea. She wasn't either.

"So, did you start with that as a good lead in to what happened with Jeremy?" she asked excitedly.

"Not exactly. But it wasn't a bust, either," I said.

Our food arrived and after I took my first few bites, I continued. "Jeremy and I had a nice conversation. He hinted at getting back together."

"Really? After four years of not even talking to each other?"

I nodded as I took another bite of my omelet.

"What? Did he see it as fate or something? I mean bumping into you in New York City like that?"

"I don't know. I think it has more to do with coincidence, from us knowing some of the same people. Sort of."

"Like six degrees of separation? Or Kevin Bacon?"

I scrunched my nose quizzically.

"You know," Chelsea continued matter-of-fact, "like the Kevin Bacon game?"

"Oh, right? The Kevin Bacon game. Jeremy is friends with Rick from their time together at the University of Texas. Rick and Wes are friends from Columbia Law School. Wes is dating you."

"Exactly," said Chelsea. "I'm connected to Wes and you. The linchpin in the whole bumping into Jeremy again." Chelsea grinned and took a sip of her coffee.

"Well, it was nice seeing him again. Even if it ended a bit awkwardly."

"That's it?" Chelsea sounded disappointed.

"Yep," I said taking another bit of my omelet. End of discussion. I hoped.

"Ashley Sullivan, there is something you are not telling me," Chelsea said leaning forward.

Am I really that transparent? Or does Chelsea just know me that well? Another bite. Another sip of orange juice.

"I know we are best friends. Sisters from another mother, really. But do you really need to know everything? Are there no secrets between us?"

"No."

"No to you don't need to know everything or no there are no secrets between us?"

"The latter," said Chelsea. "There are no secrets between us. So what gives?"

"Chels, breaking up with Brandon is still raw. I'm still wrapping my head around putting *ex* in front of *boyfriend*. I was, nonetheless, resolved in stating my position to Brandon. All-in-all, I would say that is progress. It's the best I can give you right now."

"You're right," said Chelsea. "You are absolutely correct. I'm proud of you, Ash."

"Thanks, Chels. I wouldn't be getting through this without you. And getting out last night was good for me. It was definitely better than crying on the couch and downing a carton of ice cream by myself."

"You know I push because I love you," said Chelsea as she rested her hand on my forearm.

"Yes, I know. Love you back."

I'd always have Chelsea for my best friend. I never doubted it for a second. She occupied a huge space in my life and I was grateful. While her friendship meant everything to me, not being with Brandon still stung. The hurt ran deep and healing wouldn't come easily.

Chapter 17

Chelsea and I spent Sunday afternoon shopping. That night we rented a movie and ordered takeout from a Chinese restaurant that we decided was our favorite in New York City. I spent Monday riding my bike through Central Park and curling up on the couch with a good book. There were moments where I thought of Brandon, but I fought away tears.

Despite a reasonably pleasant end to the weekend, I woke drained on Tuesday morning. The intensity of all that happened had caught up with me. Friday night seemed distant and present at the same time.

I was conflicted about my morning meeting with Brandon. The sting of his cheating and our break-up still pained me. At the same time, I couldn't deny that my attraction to him hadn't waned. I sensed that he had a control over me, one that I allowed him to have, and I didn't like it. But it was, nevertheless, real.

"Gotta run, I have an eight o'clock class," said Chelsea as she grabbed her book bag.

"I'm right behind you," I said.

We shared an elevator ride down and then parted on the street. Chelsea headed for the subway to Columbia and I grabbed a cab to the office. On the ride over I felt like I was having a mini panic attack. As soon as I arrived at work I headed for the bathroom.

I splashed cold water on my face. I felt sick to my stomach. I sprinted into a stall and offered up my breakfast. I rinsed at the sink and headed to my office. Thank goodness I had a bottle of mouthwash in my desk drawer.

"Good morning, Ashley. How was your weekend?" asked Peter, one of my social media managers.

"Fine. How was yours?" I wasn't going to get into what my weekend had really been like.

"Nice. Spent the weekend on Long Island with my folks," Peter said.

I checked the time. "Gotta run, Peter. I have an 8:30 meeting."

I closed my office door and headed down the hall. I had made the walk countless times the past three months. I had never dreaded going to Brandon's office until that morning. If I had anything left in my stomach, I probably would have been sick again. Being firm with him on the phone was one thing. Keeping my composure in person was entirely another matter.

I took a deep breath and pushed through the doors into Brandon's outer office.

Teresa was already at her desk. She looked up and smiled.

"Good morning, Ms. Sullivan."

"Good morning, Teresa. I have an 8:30 with Mr. Mitchell."

"I'll let him know you are here." She did and then told me to go on in.

I paused at Brandon's door and then walked into his office. He stood from behind his desk. His face stoic. His body rigid.

"Ashley, please sit down," he said motioning to the couch.

I froze.

"Is there a problem?" he asked.

What do you think? That was what I felt like saying. But I was going to show him that it didn't bother me. At least I was going to try to give the impression that it didn't bother me.

I walked over and sat on the couch and crossed my legs. Brandon sat in the chair opposite the couch. He tented his hands as he looked at me in silence. I figured he was gathering his thoughts.

"So, how are we going to do this?" he asked after a few moments.

"Do what, exactly?"

"Make our professional relationship work," he replied.

My stomach settled a bit. I was still anxious about the meeting, but Brandon was not confrontational. That eased my anxiety, somewhat.

"Well, it is likely to be difficult at first. But, if we focus on our jobs and continue being cordial with one another, then I think it will get easier," I offered.

"Will it get easier?"

"Brandon, you deeply hurt me. You were seeing another woman while we were dating. That sort of trumps everything else at the moment."

"Ashley, may we speak frankly on a personal basis?"

Despite my stipulation that Brandon only have professional contact, I knew that wasn't realistic. It was a way to put things off. I knew, sooner or later, we needed to address what happened.

"Yes, I suppose that we do need to have that conversation if we are to move forward professionally."

"I'm hoping that we can still have more," Brandon said as he relaxed his arms.

"I don't know, right now, if that is possible."

"Just hear me out. What you walked in on the other night was not all that it appeared to be. Yes, I admit to having gone a few dates with the woman . . ." he paused. I could tell that he was trying to decide if it was helpful to use the woman's name or not.

"Go ahead, you can say her name. If we're going to do this we should be completely free to discuss everything," I encouraged him.

The conversation was going to hurt. It was going to open a wound that hadn't even begun to heal. But better deal with it and move on.

"Jessica. She was someone I dated before you," he said. At least now I knew her name. Jessica. A pretty name. I wondered if she knew Brandon had been in a relationship?

"Did Jessica know you were in a relationship?"

"Not at first. I told her last week. So, yes, she knew when she came over the other night."

Brandon took a breath and checked my expression. I had my best poker face on. I decided to take whatever he had to say and then decide how I was going to react.

"Go on," I replied.

"Ashley, you knew I had dated a lot before you."

"Great. So being with one woman 'ties you down.' Was that the problem with us?"

"No. A moment of weakness was the problem. One time. I would never let that happen again if we were to get back together."

"A moment of weakness?" I said in disbelief.

"Ashley, I have no good explanation for what I did – "

"What you did, was date Jessica and me at the same time."

"We have already established that, Ashley. Please, let me tell you exactly what happened," he pleaded.

Brandon wasn't used to pleading. I'm not sure if he had ever pleaded before my discovering his indiscretion. I nodded for him to continue.

"Ashley, I had already told you that I never really had a serious relationship before you. I never trusted anyone completely to be with me solely because of who I am versus my money," he said as he stood and crossed his office. He looked out the window at the Manhattan skyline.

"Okay. I understand all of that. But that was all before me. I recognized it as part of your past. The problem is that it became part of your present while we were together."

"Yes. And I am truly sorry. I know I hurt you and that has pained me. Ashley, you were the first woman that I felt I could trust to be with in a real relationship. But I messed up." Brandon walked toward me and sat on the couch next to me.

"Ashley, you have to believe me that I never planned on seeing Jessica again. It doesn't excuse the fact that I did. But I knew it was wrong, and I am committed to never let it happen again. That needs to count for something."

"Perhaps. I just don't know for how much," I said as I looked at him. I could easily get lost in his beautiful blue eyes. Those eyes which so captivated me and held my gaze each time I looked into them.

"It happened two weeks after we started dating. I was at a club and had too much to drink. I ran into Jessica. She had been drinking a lot as well. She came on to me. Ashley, I was weak. I gave in to the temptation. After, I told her that it was a mistake. That I was seeing someone,, and that I was committed to the relationship. I didn't see her again until Friday night when she showed up at the penthouse."

"I'm still not sure, Brandon. And, how do you explain Friday night?"

"Apparently she still had an access card, which I took from her Friday night. I had received your text. When I came downstairs and saw the lights dimmed and the fireplace on, I assumed it was you. I was excited that you were surprising me like that. Ashley, she is the same size as you, similar hair, and it was dark enough that I couldn't make out her face from across the room. It wasn't until she threw herself at me that I noticed it wasn't you. That was just as the elevator doors opened and you saw us. I know how that sounds. I know that it would take extremely bad, and rather improbable, timing for it to happen that way. But it is the truth."

We sat in silence while I thought. I could sense Brandon's anxiety. I sensed by looking in his eyes and watching his body language that he was probably telling me the truth. But I still questioned if he could avoid another "moment of weakness" in the future.

"Although it would take incredibly small odds at such bad timing, I'm inclined to believe you," I said as I stood. "And I also tend to believe that it was just the one time with Jessica. I might, with time, even be able to forgive you. What I'm not at all confident about is it won't happen again. Maybe not with Jessica, but with one of the many other women. Or someone entirely new who you find irresistible to take out on a date. I don't know that I can trust you to be with just me."

"Ashley –"

"No. Brandon, let me say what I need to say," I interjected as I held up my hand. "Maybe I will find that level of trust again. But it is still too soon for that. I'm not ready to trust my heart to you again. Not now, anyway."

Brandon stood and stepped toward me. He took my hand in his. I let him. But I had gained a new level of clarity and strength.

"Can we go away? Find time just for the two of us?" He asked.

"Not now," I said as I let go of his hand. "Maybe not ever. I don't know."

With that I walked across his office and out the door. I headed to my office and went in and closed the door. I let out a deep breath as I sank into my chair. I honestly didn't know what my conversation with Brandon meant. Maybe I needed more time for him to gain my trust again. Maybe I was moving on from him. Only time would tell.

I decided to get some actual work done. I checked my voice mail. Most were routine business messages. Two, however, stopped me in my tracks. One was from Jeremy.

He left a sweet message which reminded me of why I had liked him so much in high school. He didn't want any awkwardness between us and hoped we could be friends. Part of his message told me that if I was ever in Los Angeles that he would arrange a private tour of the movie studio for me. That sounded like fun. I made a note to call him back later.

The second message was from a Lauren Caldwell at Adele magazine. They had taken note of what I had been doing at Jacqueline and had a similar strategy for Adele. Ms. Caldwell, as it turned out, was the Vice President of Human Resources at Adele and they wanted to offer me a job in Los Angeles.

I didn't know what to think. I didn't know what to think about Brandon, about Jeremy, or about a job offer from Adele magazine. But I had clarity about what my next move was going to be. I picked up the phone and called Lauren Caldwell.

Chapter 18

I had been offered an entry-level position with Adele when I had graduated from college. I declined the offer to take my high-profile, mega-bucks, beyond-dream job at Jacqueline fashion magazine.

But the entry-level offer was almost six months ago. A lot had changed in that short time. Adele had taken notice of my success with the Digital and Social Media strategy at Jacqueline. They wanted to steal me away so that I could do the same at Adele. I assumed the job offer would be a good one. However, I wasn't at all sure they would be willing to pay me anything close to what I was making at Jacqueline.

I nervously wrapped my fingers on my desk as the phone rang. I was returning Lauren Caldwell's call. I was intrigued at what the offer might be.

Was the universe somehow trying to tell me that I had a future in Los Angeles? A future without Brandon Mitchell and Jacqueline? A future that could include Jeremy due to an amazing job opportunity at Adele? Did I even want that?

On the third ring my call was answered.

"Lauren Caldwell," answered the voice on the other end of the phone.

"Ms. Caldwell, this is Ashley Sullivan returning your call," I said.

"Yes, Ms. Sullivan. Thank you for returning my call. I know that I didn't leave any details, but I hope that this is more than a courtesy call to decline discussing an offer," Ms. Caldwell said.

"To be honest, I'm not sure of my intentions. I'm interested in learning more about your offer," I replied.

"Well, that is an encouraging start. We'd like to bring you out to Los Angeles to visit the office. We want you to meet the staff and have your questions answered. It will also give us an opportunity to present our formal offer to you. What I can tell you, is we are prepared to beat your current salary and benefits package," explained Ms. Caldwell.

"I haven't shared what my current salary and benefits package is," I said.

"Let's just say that we have a pretty good ballpark figure on what it is and how we are prepared to entice you with a sweeter offer," she replied.

Perhaps I was still a bit naive but I wasn't clear on how Adele would have any idea about what I made. They were a private company. Jacqueline was part of a private company. And the two magazines were fierce competitors. I decided not to dwell on it.

"I appreciate that very much. I must admit that I am flattered in your level of interest. I also feel I should tell you I am happy at Jacqueline. I am happy living in Manhattan."

"We expected that to be the case. We also believe that if you visit with us and see all that we have to offer, a position at Adele will be very attractive. If nothing else, you can get an all-expenses paid getaway to L.A. for a few days," she said in completing her pitch to me.

"It would be hard for me to get away during the week with everything I have scheduled right now. A trip would also raise questions here that I am not prepared to address at the moment. I would like to explore this option with you further, but not at the risk of my current position," I replied.

"Understood. We were thinking that we would have you out over the weekend. The key staff have already agreed to meet with you on Saturday. Ms. Sullivan, we all believe you would be a tremendous asset at Adele. We are willing to accommodate you as much as possible."

As Lauren Caldwell spoke, I was finding fewer reasons not to go. A weekend getaway on the other side of the country might be just what the doctor ordered. I agreed to meeting with Adele that coming weekend.

"Excellent news," said Ms. Caldwell. "Give us a few hours to finalize the plans and I will email you all the details later today."

"That sounds fine. I look forward to meeting you this weekend," I said.

"The pleasure will be all of ours. See you Saturday."

My head was spinning. I wasn't sure how I felt about the trip. I was both excited and burdened with a tinge of guilt.

Jacqueline had been very good to me. I was paid amazingly well, had a fabulous apartment that I shared with my best friend, and generally enjoyed living in Manhattan. The only thing that soured the whole experience was the state of things with Brandon. My relationship with Brandon had been amazing, and then he cheated. That fact complicated everything.

I reasoned that I owed it to myself to explore my options. Once I knew what the situation at Adele looked like, I could compare that to my experience at Jacqueline. Maybe seeing Jeremy while I was in Los Angeles would also give another point of reference with respect to my personal life. I decided that going to Los Angeles for the weekend was a good choice. I'd decide on the rest later.

Chapter 19

Chelsea and I sat down to dinner at our kitchen table. I had picked up a pizza from the pizzeria around the corner from our apartment. Half cheese and half anchovy. I loved anchovies. Chelsea hated them.

I had a flashback to all the times I had shared a pizza with Phil Reed. Half anchovy and half pepperoni. No one in my life ever wanted anchovies on their half of the pizza.

"Wow, Ash. Is it a real serious offer?" Chelsea picked up a piece of cheese pizza and put it on her plate.

"It sure seems to be. I'll know better this weekend," I answered. I took a bite of my anchovy pizza.

Chelsea made her yuck face at me.

"I'd hate to see you move that far away, but if the job is that amazing then it may not be a bad thing for you. A fresh start."

"I'd miss you to pieces," I said, "but we can visit each other often. Especially if I'm making even more than I do now. And don't worry about the apartment. I can take care of the rent until the lease is up," I offered.

I didn't want to force Chelsea to have to find a new apartment during the school year. I also knew that she'd need to find something much smaller and not nearly as nice, even if she found a roommate.

"But, we don't need to worry about any of that right now. Let's cross that bridge when we come to it. I may not even take the job."

"Now you listen to me, Ashley Sullivan. I don't want you spending one second thinking about me or what I will do.

Living in this fabulous apartment with you has been a real gift. You know it still makes me feel weird not contributing to the rent. You make the best decision for you. Period."

Chelsea was the greatest BFF in the world. She always thought of me first. She always had my back. The biggest downside to a possible move to Los Angeles would be moving away from her. She'd been in my life since the first day of college and now I couldn't imagine a day without her.

"Have you decided whether you are going to call Jeremy?" Chelsea asked as she polished off her first slice of pizza.

"I'm thinking I will. I checked the itinerary for Adele and I'll have Saturday night and all of Sunday free. I have the vacation days so I decided to take next Monday off and fly back then. A long weekend, after what I have gone through, won't raise any suspicions at the office."

"So, do you think you will see Jeremy in LA?" Chelsea asked rather hopefully.

"I haven't given that part much thought. Not this weekend. I know that much. There is too much I am trying to process. It would just complicate things further," I said.

"Complicate or offer a nice distraction?" Chelsea pressed.

"Complicate," I reiterated.

"But you're not ruling it out altogether?"

"No. But it's not like I'm making plans for it either. Like everything else in my life right now, I'll just have to wait and see what happens."

"I think you should call him and get together."

"I'll take your comment under advisement. Now, tell me, how are things going with Wes?"

Chelsea had been dating Wesley exclusively for nearly a month. Not that this was a first for her, but she seemed to like him better than any guy she had ever dated before. She smiled at the mention of his name.

"He's really great. Handsome, smart, funny. I think this one has a chance of being a healthy, long-term relationship."

"Well, I certainly hope so. You deserve it," I said.

I picked up another piece of anchovy pizza and took a big bite.

"Yuck. I'll never get you liking anchovies," she said as she turned up her nose.

"I think you've said that before," I replied.

"Just as true now as it was before," Chelsea said.

I realized some things were constant in my life. I was grateful for them. It made the changes swirling around me a little easier to deal with. I hoped that would keep me moving forward and making the best decisions.

Chapter 20

I managed to get through the rest of the week by keeping busy with current projects. Thankfully, Brandon was out of town on business. Knowing that he wasn't around the office made my week easier. I left early on Friday afternoon to leave plenty of time to get to the airport for my flight to Los Angeles.

I made it through security and settled into a seat at the gate. Adele had spared no expense for my trip. I had a first-class ticket, and they booked me a suite at a fancy hotel near their office. I knew for certain that the offer would be serious.

A family piled into the seats near me. I heard them before I saw them. Two parents with three out-of-control kids. I only hoped that they were sitting at the very back of the plane. I was especially thankful that I would be in first class.

I popped in my ear buds and selected a Josh Groban play list. His voice carried me away from the hysterical parents trying to gain control of their unruly kids. I was part way through track three when I heard the boarding call for first-class passengers. I made my way toward the gate. After boarding, I settled into the plush and spacious seat.

Champagne, cheese, and crackers were served. The family from the waiting area scurried past. I watched as they made their way to the back of the plane and out of hearing range. I smiled and eased back into my seat.

After dinner I drifted off to sleep. I woke just in time to prepare for our landing into LAX. It was almost 8:30 pm LA time.

After we landed I made my way off the plane and to ground transportation. Adele had sent a car service to pick me up and bring me to my hotel. The driver was friendly and had a nice southern California tan.

Upon arriving at the hotel, the first thing I noticed in the lobby were all the pictures of famous people who frequented the hotel. Wondering if any of them had ever stayed in my room, I checked in and made my way upstairs to my suite. Very nice furnishings. Plus, I had an amazing view of the Los Angeles skyline.

I showered and put on a pair of comfy pajamas. When I wasn't trying to sex it up, I preferred my pajamas with sheep on them. I padded across the suite and pulled out a package of materials that Adele had put together for me. Adele was second only to Jacqueline in sales and prestige. It was also clear that they intended to be number one before long.

I felt a little funny having this information. I was, after all, an executive at Jacqueline. Adele was going to play hardball in wooing me to their team. I was flattered, to be sure. But I had mixed emotions about it. Only natural I suppose.

My phone rang. It was Lauren Caldwell.

"Welcome to L.A., Ms. Sullivan. How was your flight?" she asked as I answered the phone.

"It was fine. Thank you," I replied.

"Wonderful. Have you settled into your hotel yet?"

"Yes. It is absolutely lovely."

"I'm glad that you like it," Ms. Caldwell said. "Please enjoy a leisurely breakfast in the morning. I just want to confirm that the car will be at the hotel to pick you up at 11:00 am to bring you to the office."

"Yes. Thank you. I'm looking forward to our day together tomorrow," I replied.

"As are we. Sleep well and we will see you tomorrow," she said.

"Thank you. Good night," I said.

"Good night," said Ms. Caldwell before we ended our call.

I returned to reading the Adele materials. When I finished, I decided to watch some of the Tonight Show Starring Jimmy Fallon. I had always loved Jimmy Fallon and was enjoying him as host of the iconic late night show. A perfect choice, I thought.

After a little television, I read a few chapters in a new romance I had downloaded to my Kindle. It was so good that I had trouble putting it down. Some of the scenes reminded me of Brandon. I wanted to smile and cry at the same time.

I decided on sleep instead. I had a full day ahead of me and I wanted to be well rested. I snuggled under the Egyptian Cotton sheets and drifted off to sleep.

Chapter 21

I had a nice breakfast in the hotel restaurant. I thought I had spotted George Clooney in the restaurant, but I couldn't be sure. As I waited in the lobby for the car service to arrive I was keeping an eye out for celebrities. The car arrived, and I left without any more celebrity sightings.

The ride to Adele was only about fifteen minutes. I'm not sure that we traveled all that far, but the traffic was heavy for a Saturday morning. The driver told me that a section of the block was shut down for a movie crew. It had everything all tied up.

As we pulled up to Adele, I was impressed by the building. It was a modern glass structure that glistened in the California sunshine. A woman was waiting for me as I stepped out of the back of the towne car. I assumed it was Lauren Caldwell.

"Lauren Caldwell," the woman said as she extended her hand. "It is a pleasure to meet you, Ms. Sullivan."

She had a broad and warm smile. She was my height and looked to be in her early forties. She was slender and fit. A runner's physique.

"Thank you. It's nice to meet you as well," I replied as we shook hands.

"Let me escort you upstairs and introduce you to Ronald Vargas. He is our Vice President of Business Development. He will give you a tour of the office and discuss how your proposed position fits into the magazine's strategy."

The marble lobby was spacious and had a large, modern reception desk. Being a Saturday, the lobby was empty. Lauren

Caldwell led me to the elevator, and we traveled to the executive floor.

Ronald Vargas greeted us as we exited the elevator.

"Ms. Sullivan. Thank you for agreeing to give up your weekend to meet with us," he said as we shook hands.

"Thank you for accommodating my schedule," I replied.

"Well, I'll leave you two for now. I will meet up with you in a few hours," said Lauren Caldwell as she headed down the hall toward her office.

Ron Vargas was slightly taller than me. He was in his early fifties and carried a few extra pounds. He had a friendly, round face. He reminded me of a cherub.

He moved surprisingly fast. I felt like we were power walking our way through the tour. I didn't sense that he was trying to rush me. I got the impression that this was his normal speed.

The office was nice. Similar to Jacqueline's office back in Manhattan. Mr. Vargas pointed out where all the departments were. When we reached his office, we went inside and sat down. He explained what Adele hoped to accomplish with their Digital and Social Media department.

They had a department, and it was functioning. This was more than existed when I was hired at Jacqueline. Mr. Vargas further explained that they were committing significant resources to expand and improve the department. In fact, the Digital publication was getting a complete face lift. What they needed was talent to head the department.

He explained that the former head of the department took a position at a new tech company. It was rather sudden and came at an inopportune time. They had, naturally, been monitoring what we had been doing at Jacqueline. They wanted me to come to Adele and replicate that success.

We talked at length about the company, the department, and all that my position would entail. They would give me a lot of latitude to restructure the department as I saw fit. They were willing to spend at least 15% more on the department than I currently had in my department's budget at Jacqueline.

I was impressed with what I heard. Ronald Vargas was easy to speak with. He insisted that I call him Ron. He told me that all his friends called him Ron, and he thought we could be good friends. I took him as completely sincere.

Adele had a friendly feel to it. And they were hungry. They were hungry to take the top spot in the fashion media world. They were convinced that I would play a pivotal role in getting them there.

After Ron and I finished meeting, he introduced me to the Digital and Social Media staff. They were knowledgeable, driven, and seemed genuinely excited in the prospect that I might head their future efforts. I figured they would kiss up a bit to a potential new boss, but it didn't seem that way to me. I liked the staff and could easily see myself working with them.

When Ron and I finished meeting the staff, he brought me to Lauren Caldwell's office. They had made lunch reservations at Spago Beverly Hills. I had several of Wolfgang Puck's cooking products, but I had never eaten at one of his restaurants.

When we arrived at Spago's, we had a booth near the wine wall. I was amazed at all the bottles of wine. The restaurant was modern and elegant. The food and wine were excellent. From what I had experienced so far, I could get use to L.A..

Ron, Lauren Caldwell, and I had pleasant conversation over lunch. When it came time for dessert, they decided it was time to reel me in.

"Ashley, it should come as no surprise how much we want you to be part of the Adele family," said Ron with a warm smile.

"It has been a pleasant day. It does feel like a family," I said in all honesty.

"We are pleased that you feel that way," said Lauren. We, too, were now on a fist name basis.

"I know that I mentioned on the phone that we were prepared to beat your current salary and benefits. I think that you will agree we have done that with this offer," she said as she handed me a folded piece of letterhead.

I opened the piece of paper. My eyes grew as wide as the moon. They offered me 10% more than I was currently making. I already felt like I was making so much money. The offer was unreal.

The benefits were equal to or better than what I currently had. They would pay all my moving costs, including covering the remainder of my lease in Manhattan. I was speechless. Then I was breathless. If I signed a contract within one week I would receive a generous signing bonus equal to two months of the proposed salary.

Ron and Lauren looked expectantly at each other and then back to me. They had done everything they could to impress me. They also knew the offer was superb. The only question was, whether or not I wanted to take the job and move to Los Angeles. I took a deep breath and exhaled.

"This is an extraordinary offer. I don't quite know what to say."

"We hope that you will say 'yes,'" said Ron as he smiled at me.

"This has been a lovely day. I am truly impressed with Adele and what you want to accomplish. I am beyond flattered in your interest in me. I need a little time to process everything before I make my final decision."

Ron and Lauren clearly hoped that I would say 'yes' on the spot, but they must have expected I would need some time to make my decision. They were gracious and warm for the remainder of our time together. They asked my plans for the evening and I told them that I would be visiting with a friend who lived in the city.

I agreed to be in touch with them as soon as I made my decision. I indicated that I would get back to them before the end of the following week.

The car service took me from the restaurant to my hotel. I had the rest of the afternoon before Jeremy would pick me up for dinner. I changed into my bathing suit and headed to the pool for a swim. I figured some laps would clear my mind and help me think.

Chapter 22

After a nice swim I went back to my hotel room and showered. I put on the soft hotel robe and padded to the comfy chair in the corner of the room. I called my parents to fill them in on the job offer and get their opinion.

They were both over the moon about the job offer. They also liked the idea of the shorter flight between Austin and Los Angeles vs. the longer flight to New York. But they also wanted me to consider where my heart was in all of it. They shared a story with me that they never had before.

When they were dating, my dad had cheated on my mom with an old girlfriend. I was floored. That didn't sound like my dad at all. He loved my mom so unconditionally. He would never do anything to hurt her.

The situation wasn't exactly the same as with Brandon, but they offered it to me for whatever it was worth. My parents had been dating for several months and had a terrible argument. They hadn't broken up over it, but they were both steaming. They didn't speak for a week.

It was during that week it happened. My dad fell into the arms of a former girlfriend. My dad confessed to my mother, and they broke up. After a few months, and a lot of tears and talking it out, my parents got back together. The rest, as they say, is history. They built an incredibly strong relationship. They were married two years later. Nine months after that I came along. My sister three years later.

My parents have been happily married for over 22 years. They always seemed the perfect couple. They provided an amazing family life for my sister and me. Their point, which wasn't lost on me, was they would have missed out on all of it if they hadn't worked through my dad's one very bad decision. It took a lot for my mom to forgive him, but she did.

They weren't condoning what my father, or Brandon, had done. And they weren't saying that everyone could, or even should, get back together. What they wanted me to know was it worked for them. But they had to make it work. And they both wanted to make it work.

After I got over the initial shock of what they told me, it certainly gave me even more to think about. The difference, I stated, was that my dad was, at his core, a one woman kind of guy. Yes, he made a terrible decision during a time of emotional upheaval in their relationship. It didn't excuse his actions, but it was out of character.

Brandon, on the other hand, had made a practice of dating a long list of women. His was a relapse to what he knew best. It was very much in character for him. Then my mother said something that gave me pause.

"Perhaps, then, he needs more time to learn how to be with one woman. Assuming that he wants to do that. And, that it is with the right woman," she said.

"So, are you suggesting that I should give Brandon a pass?"

"No. What I am saying is maybe one relapse does not predict a trend. Ashley, dear, you are a smart and together young woman. You need to look at the entire situation. Think with your head and follow your heart," replied my mom.

"And what do you think of Jeremy Wagner?" I asked my parents.

They both told me how much they liked Jeremy. The Wagners were a wonderful family. They were happy when I dated him in high school. I told them I was seeing him, as friends, while I was in L.A.

"Well, my advice remains the same, dear," said my mom. "Professionally, I don't think you can make a wrong decision. You have a fabulous career already. Adele would be more money, but, my goodness, you are already doing so well. I think you need to decide where your heart is. Ultimately, that is where you will find happiness."

The conversation was much deeper than I had expected, but it helped. My parents gave me a lot to think about. They confirmed that I needed to look at my situation from all angles. Ultimately, however, what did I want for myself?

They ended our phone call with some very good news. My dad would be starting as a Math teacher of record on Monday. It meant he would be earning a salary and benefits while he completed his teacher certification program.

He had a degree in Mathematics and there was a shortage of math teachers in Texas. He started a teacher certification program and had been interviewing with local school districts. I was thrilled.

My dad was great at explaining math. My sister and I never would have made it through our math classes without his help. He'd be a great teacher.

"I won't be making what I did before, but the salary and benefits are certainly enough for us. We are going to be just fine," said my dad.

Then he choked up as he thanked me for my financial help. They were able to keep the house, their insurance, and send my younger sister off to college.

I told them that I could continue to help if need be. My parents told me that wouldn't be necessary. I decided that I would send them on a nice vacation. They couldn't turn that down. Not if it was already paid for.

When I got off the phone with my parents I called Chelsea. She was excited to learn about my job offer. Even if it meant that I might move to Los Angeles.

She could see the point my parents were making, but I think that Chelsea liked the idea of my exploring something with Jeremy. But, in the end, she wanted me to be happy. She'd support me no matter what my decision was.

I finished my call with Chelsea and got dressed for dinner with Jeremy. I put on a nice pair of jeans and a casual blouse. We agreed that it would be casual and light. I had been refreshed by my swim. Maybe a fun evening with Jeremy was just what I needed.

Chapter 23

Jeremy picked me up, and we went for dinner at a small Italian restaurant near my hotel. He was wearing dark jeans and a polo shirt. He smelled of a pleasant cologne. I was determined that we were just going out as friends. But he was rather fetching.

"So, what's good here?" I asked Jeremy as we looked over our menus.

"The Chicken Parmesan is outstanding. But everything is good," he replied.

"Actually, the Chicken Parm sounds perfect," I said as I closed my menu and placed it to the side.

"I think we'll make that two Chicken parms. It's my favorite dish here," he said with a smile. He had a nice smile. I caught myself staring at his mouth. Other than Brandon, he was the best kisser I ever dated.

"So, tell me how your meeting went at Adele," he said as he placed his napkin in his lap.

I recounted my day. I didn't share the details of the salary, but told him that it was a very attractive offer.

The waiter brought us our wine and a basket of freshly baked bread. He took our dinner order and retreated to the kitchen. Jeremy raised his wine glass. I followed for a toast.

"Here's to an attractive job offer. And to dinner with an old friend," said Jeremy. We touched glasses and took a sip of our wine.

"Ooh, this is tasty," I said.

"It's their house special. It goes great with the Chicken Parmesan," he said. "When do you need to give Adele your decision?"

"They gave me a week if I wanted to receive a signing bonus. I could probably have more time than that, without a bonus, but it was certainly intended that I let them know within a week," I answered.

"Do you know which way you are leaning?"

"I really don't. I liked the people I met at Adele. I think they are a great company and I could be happy there."

"It certainly sounds like they want you."

"It's flattering. Most people would probably say that I'd be crazy not to take the job. But, I already have a great job that I love."

"I, for one, would love to see you move out here. It would be nice to have a friend from home in L.A.."

"You're sweet," I said. "How do you like living here?"

"I like it. The traffic can be a bear, but you learn to adjust your schedule to account for it. The weather is great."

We chatted casually about how Jeremy found living in L.A.. He shared some of his favorite places to go and things to do. The entire time, however, I felt that he was a little nervous. I sensed he was hoping our evening would turn into more than friends.

I had already told myself that nothing was going to happen. I wondered if I could allow myself to question that decision. Even overturn it? Is that what I even wanted?

Too many questions. Not enough answers. If only my heart knew what it wanted. Why did Jeremy have to be so nice and so cute?

Thankfully, our dinner arrived. It allowed us to talk casually while we concentrated on our meals. When we finished eating, and the waiter had cleared our table, Jeremy let out a deep breath.

"Ashley, I know what we said the last time we were together . . ." he began.

"Jeremy, wait," I said. "I think I know what you are going to say. I don't want to lead you on in any way. You are a wonderful guy. But right now, I don't know what decision I am going to make. If I take the job at Adele . . ., well, maybe we can revisit what our relationship can be beyond friends. I just don't know what I want right now and that wouldn't be fair to you."

"It's Brandon, isn't it?" Jeremy asked.

"Yes. I'm trying to work out if I can trust my heart to him again. I'm trying to figure out if he is the man I truly want to be with."

"You're right. I'm sorry that I even brought it up. I hope I didn't ruin the evening."

"No. Not at all. Dinner was lovely. It's nice seeing you," I said. "Jeremy, if I wasn't trying to sort all of this out. . ."

"You don't need to say any more. I get it."

"How about dessert?" I asked.

Jeremy agreed, and we enjoyed our dessert and a cup of coffee.

We walked back to my hotel. I gave Jeremy a hug in the lobby and thanked him for dinner. I told him I would let him know what I decided about the job. Regardless of my decision, we agreed to keep in touch.

I watched Jeremy leave the hotel lobby. There was a part of me that could see myself with him. I just wasn't convinced it was a big enough part of me.

Chapter 24

I went back to my room and slipped out of my clothes. I washed my face and brushed my teeth. I pulled out my pajamas and put them on. My cellphone rang.

I picked it up. It was Brandon. My pulse quickened. I was trying to decide if I should answer.

"Hello," I said.

"Ashley, I heard that you are out of town until late Monday. Is everything okay?"

"Yes. Everything is fine. I just needed a long weekend away."

"To think?" he asked.

I didn't want to lie. I also couldn't tell him that I had visited Adele and was considering a job offer. I was away. And I was thinking about things. So, I guess I could answer 'yes.'"

"For the most part. Some distance does help."

"How much distance?" he asked.

"If you want to know where I am, why don't you just ask?"

"Would you tell me?"

"Probably not."

"That's why I didn't ask."

I had to smile at the remark. I sat in the comfy chair and crossed my legs. "Criss-cross Applesauce" a teacher had once said about sitting in a circle for story time. Strange how, and when, certain things come back to you.

"So you figured you would ask a series of leading questions to figure it out?"

"Seemed like a good as plan as any," Brandon said. "Look, Ashley, I'm worried about you. I want to know you are alright."

"I think that 'alright' is a bit relative for me right now. I'm getting through my days and trying to come to some decisions," I offered.

"Do any of those decisions include us?"

I paused for a moment. How much did I want to get into this at that moment? Was I ready to have another conversation with Brandon about 'us'?

"It's part of a larger whole," I finally said.

"Are you thinking of leaving your job?" he asked. I doubted he knew about my meeting with Adele or their offer. But he was a smart businessman. He read people extremely well. It was probably only natural, given the situation, that I might consider working somewhere else.

He could tell that I was hesitating.

"You don't have to answer that," he said to break the silence. "Just be honest with me. Are you doing okay? At least okay enough?"

"Yes. Okay enough." That was the absolute truth. I wasn't particularly happy. I wouldn't even say that I was content. But life wasn't terrible either. Could be much worse. Okay enough seemed about right.

"Well, I guess that has to be good enough. At least for now," he said.

"I guess," I said. I missed him. Hearing his voice and the genuine concern he expressed made me realize it. I still didn't know if I could be with him again, but I did miss him.

"I should let you go. Enjoy the rest of your long weekend. I hope you have a chance to figure some things out." I could tell that he didn't want to get off the phone. He almost seemed vulnerable.

"Brandon?"

"Yes?"

"Are you doing okay?"

There was some silence on the phone as he paused to consider my question. I don't think he was expecting it. I'm not sure I planned on asking it. But I did want to know.

"I'm doing . . . okay enough," he replied.

"I'm in Los Angeles," I offered. I didn't know what else to say, and I didn't want the call to end. The thought of hanging up and being alone in my hotel room made me feel not just alone, but lonely.

Maybe what my parents had said earlier was influencing my decision. Maybe it was the direction I had always been moving in. Probably a little of both. What I felt was that I wasn't ready to let go of Brandon. Maybe my heart could risk be broken again if it meant a chance of finding lasting happiness with him.

"You could come to L.A.," I suggested.

"Is that what you really want?" he asked.

"Long term? I still need to figure that out. But I want to see you. I want to take a step toward you."

"Where are you staying?"

"The Grand Hotel."

"I can be there in under an hour."

"What? You are in L.A.?"

"Yes. I can explain when I get there. Assuming you want me to come over."

"I'll see you when you get here. Room 735."

"I'm glad you want to see me. I want to make all of this right between us. See you in a little while."

We ended our call. I felt a rush of excitement. I was curious as to why Brandon was in Los Angeles, but that was secondary. A distant second to the fact that I would be with him within the hour.

I was a bit anxious, so I put on the television to occupy my time until he arrived. I flipped through the channels and couldn't find anything that I wanted to watch. I left the TV on some documentary about cats. It ranged from lions and tigers to domestic kitties.

After about forty-five minutes I heard a knock at the door. I turned off the television and padded over to the door. I peeked through the peep hole. I assumed it was Brandon, but you can never be too safe. I instantly honed in on Brandon's dreamy blue eyes and his gorgeous face. He had a five o'clock shadow that looked great on him.

I opened the door, and he stepped in. I closed the door behind him. He was unsure how to greet me, so I stretched up and gave him a kiss on the cheek.

He looked amazing. As he always did. He was wearing khaki pants and a New York Yankees t-shirt.

"It's wonderful to see you, Ashley. I've missed you."

"Let's sit," I said motioning to the couch in the sitting area. "Do you want anything to drink?"

"No, thank you. I like the pajamas," he remarked with a warm smile.

"I wasn't planning on entertaining anyone this weekend."

"Ashley, you look cute in whatever you have on."

"I'm glad you are here, but why are you here? In L.A., I mean?" I asked after we sat down next to each other on the couch.

"To be honest, I came in hopes that you would want to see me."

"You came to L.A. just to see me? How did you know I was here? You're not bugging me or having me followed, are you?"

"A lot of questions there, Ashley. Yes, I did come to L.A. in hopes of seeing you. If you didn't want to see me, I would have gone back to New York. No, I am not bugging you, nor am I having you followed."

"Then, how did you know I would be here? Did you talk to Chelsea?"

"No. I did not speak with Chelsea. I get the distinct impression she is not fond of me at the moment."

"That would be true."

"I have to admit, she frightens me a little."

"Don't feel bad, she has that effect on a lot of people. But only when she wants to. She is also a real sweetheart. You just don't want to cross her. You crossed her by hurting me."

Brandon simply nodded in agreement with everything I had said.

"Ashley, I knew you were in L.A. because I heard about your meeting at Adele. I'm not upset about that. In fact, I will fight to keep you at Jacqueline. Regardless of what happens between us personally, you are too vital to the company to let you walk away."

"How did you know I was meeting with Adele? I can't imagine it would be in their interest for you to find out before I accepted their offer."

"They didn't tell me. Not formally. At our levels, the fashion media world is relatively small. People like to gossip. It is practically impossible for an executive at one magazine to meet with another magazine without the rumor mill starting to churn."

"I guess I never thought much about that. You have to understand that they contacted me. If things hadn't been the way they are between us, I would have flat out rejected a meeting or any offer. But, given our situation, I figured it didn't hurt to explore my options."

"I understand. And, like I said, I will fight to keep you. That part is business, and it is good for my business to have you employed at Jacqueline and not our competition. So, whatever they have offered I will beat it. I hope it will be enough to convince you to stay."

"I haven't made a decision. But that is good to know." I paused a few beats. "It isn't about the job."

"I know," Brandon said.

"Brandon, it's always been about us. Whether I can trust you again. Whether I can risk you hurting me again."

"I can't promise you will never get hurt. In the same way you can't promise you will never hurt me. Relationships aren't all roses and champagne. But I will never cheat on you again. That I do promise."

"So, you want a relationship with me? You are willing to work at a completely honest relationship? Committed to just me?"

"Yes. Ashley, I hate that I hurt you like I did. I've been a mess without you. From the very beginning I have been infatuated with you. I hoped you could be the woman I would want to settle down with. And you were. You are."

We were silent for a moment. Brandon wanted to let what he had said sink in. I needed time to process everything.

"I never regretted being in a relationship with you. Seeing Jessica again was a mistake. A mistake I will never make again. Not with her, not with any other woman. I only want to be with you. Ashley, I love you."

Neither of us had said those three words to each other before. I had felt them, but I was afraid to say them for fear of driving Brandon away too soon. But now he had said them first. I LOVE YOU. The most powerful three words in the English language.

"I love you, too."

Chapter 25

"I love you, but that is not a totally new feeling. It doesn't mean that everything is just okay between us like nothing happened," I said as I placed my hand on his.

"What does it mean, then?"

"It means we have come a long way from where we were. It means we can try. I am going to give you a second chance. But under my terms."

"Name them."

"Number one, no other women. That should go without saying, but . . ."

"Understood."

"Number two, we have to be completely in the open with our relationship. I think most everybody had it figured out, but I don't want there to be any question about who your girlfriend is."

"I agree completely."

"Number three, I will be watching you like a hawk. Chelsea will be watching you like a hawk. I think I can convince your grandmother to watch you like a hawk. If you slip up, we are through forever."

"Forever is a long time."

"Then don't slip up."

"Number four, you will need to at least match Adele's offer in both my salary and my department's budget. I am remaining at Jacqueline. It is where I want to be professionally and personally. But, consider it a small payment for your indiscretion."

"Done."

"Wait. I'm not quite finished yet. Out of your personal funds, you will donate the two months salary signing bonus I would have received from Adele to the charity of my choice. And you will continue to do so every quarter."

Brandon waited a few moments to make sure I was finished. "You are a tough negotiator Ashley Sullivan," he said with a grin.

"You did once tell me you liked assertive Ashley."

Brandon nodded his head in complete agreement. Not that he had much choice if he wanted us to get back together.

"Finally," I said, "this is a trial basis. Prove to me you can faithfully commit and we can move on to a future together."

"Okay. So, am I on the clock, so to speak?"

"Hold on a second," I said as I raised my hand. "Do you understand the terms?"

"Yes. They are crystal clear."

"And you agree to them?"

"Yes. Without question."

I tilted my head at him. "Hmm. You don't even want to know what this is costing you? Financially, I mean? You don't even know what the offer from Adele was. Or do you?"

"No. I don't. And it doesn't matter. It is a bargain, at any price, to keep you at Jacqueline. And, more importantly, to have you back in my life."

I leaned over and kissed him. He wrapped me in his arms and I nestled my head against his chest. We stayed like that for quite some time.

I was happy to take it all in. I was not in any rush to leave, or speak, or think about anything. This had been an important turning point. I only hoped it would lead to the relationship and life I knew was possible with Brandon.

After some time of gazing out over the downtown Los Angeles skyline, we went to dinner. We ate and talked and laughed. It was the old Brandon. Actually, an improved version of the old Brandon. I was feeling comfortable with him again.

"How would you like to go to France?" Brandon asked half way through our meal.

"I'd love to go to France. Business, pleasure, or both?"

"Strictly pleasure. I've wanted to take you since we met. Now seems like a very good time for us to get away for a romantic vacation."

"Now, as in . . ."

"Now, as in tomorrow. We can fly home to New York tonight and leave for Paris in the morning."

"Can we just pick up and go like that?"

"Why not? I've already had Teresa clear my schedule for next week. Your staff is humming along. We can both afford a week out of the office. I think it would be good for us."

"I'm not one to argue with a week in France. Let's do it."

"Fabulous. I was thinking part of the week cruising the French Riviera and then top it off with a few days in Paris."

"Sounds magical."

I was as giddy as a school girl. I had always wanted to go to France. Now, I was going at the most perfect time. Brandon and I were rekindling the spark of our relationship. Better than that, we had, for the first time, told each other "I love you."

We finished dinner, gathered our luggage, and I checked out of the hotel. Brandon called a car service to take us to the airport. His Learjet was ready and waiting to take us to New York.

When we landed in New York I texted Chelsea and let her know that I was coming home a little early from L.A.. I left out any details. She was going to flip out when I told her what was going on.

Brandon had one of the company cars pick us up and drive us to our buildings. As I made my way through the lobby of my building, Chelsea came up beside me. I jumped.

"Hey, Ash. Just got your text."

"Don't sneak up on me like that. A great way to get yourself pepper sprayed."

"Sorry. Why are you home early? Everything okay?"

"I guess that depends on your perspective."

"Uh oh. I don't think I'm going to like this," Chelsea said as we stepped onto the elevator.

I wasn't sure that I wanted to tell her with nowhere to run.

"Let's get upstairs and let me go to the bathroom and then I'll tell you everything."

"You're stalling. I'm definitely not going to like it."

There was no use in pretending with Chelsea. She could read me like a book. But if she didn't have any details, she couldn't lay into me too hard.

After we arrived at our apartment I made a beeline for the bathroom. I drank a lot of water on the flight back and really did have to go pretty bad. Chelsea was sitting on my bed waiting for me.

"Alright, Ashley. Give."

"I have decided to stay at Jacqueline. In fact, I will be staying with an increase in salary to match the offer from Adele." I said feeling rather proud of myself.

"That's wonderful. I am so glad you're staying!"

Chelsea jumped up and gave me a big hug. Then she realized there had to be more. The part she was not going to like.

"Okay. That is the good news. What is the part I am not going to like?"

"I think it is also a good thing. I'm taking a little vacation to France. I leave tomorrow."

"Whoa. That's . . .great. Do I take it you are not going to France alone?"

"You'd be correct."

"Since you are staying in New York, I somehow doubt you have miraculously fallen in love with Jeremy and are going with him."

"Also correct."

Chelsea crossed her arms and stiffened her back. Her eyes bore into me. I was glad she couldn't shoot lasers with her eyes.

"Brandon?"

"Yes."

Chelsea tapped her foot rapidly. Her body tensed. I don't even think she realized.

"I need to sit," she said as she plopped back onto my bed. She sat in silence.

I let her. I figured it was better than getting into an argument. Although I suspected one might already be brewing.

"Well?!" she finally said.

"Well, what?"

"How did it happen? How did you go from where you were Friday to where it seems you are now? Which I am not entirely clear on. Other than you are jetting off to France with Brandon."

"To be honest, I think I had been leaning this way all along. I didn't know it, but it became clearer to me. Brandon and I have had some wonderful heart to heart conversations."

"Do you trust him?"

"Conditionally, for now. I've laid out terms to our giving this another try."

I explained the terms to Chelsea. I told her all about my conversations with Brandon.

Chelsea's mood softened somewhat.

"I can't say that this surprises me," she stated. "I am glad that you told him I would be watching him like a hawk. And I will be. Believe me, Ash, when I tell you he better not even come close to breaking your heart again."

"I know you will. And I know you have your concerns about this, Chels. But I really need you to support my decision."

I sat down on my bed next to her. "I do love him. I know that to be true. I'm willing to take this chance because my life is better with him in it. It is something I have learned through all of this."

Chelsea hugged me. "I luv ya, Ash. You know I will support you. I want you to be happy. I've also got your back. Always."

"I know. I luv ya, too. I'm happy with where I think things are headed. I couldn't have said that last week."

"Okay, so tell me about France. What are we going to need to pack for you?"

"French Riviera and then a few days in Paris."

"Love it! I have a few ideas."

"I thought you might." I smiled at where I was at in my life. I felt this vacation to France would tell me a lot about what to expect going forward. But I was glad to be traveling this road now.

Chapter 26

The French Riviera was gorgeous. We were still recovering from jet lag, albeit jet lag from traveling on Brandon's private jet, so we were lounging on the deck of Jacqueline III, the Davenport family yacht. Well, one of them. The yacht they kept in Europe. They had others in the Caribbean, California, and the Hamptons.

It was hard for me to get used to all the luxury. I know it may sound strange, but I grew up very middle class. We had everything we needed and enough of what we wanted. But we only saw toys like the Davenport yachts in the distance when we would go to the beach on South Padre Island. Yet, here I was sunning myself on the deck of Jacqueline III in the French Riviera. Pinch me.

"What a beautiful day," Brandon said. "Warmer than usual this time of year," he added as he slid a deck chair over near me. He kissed me on the cheek and plopped into his chair.

"It is so peaceful. I could just stay here forever," I said.

"A nice start to our little get away." Brandon took my hand in his.

"Most definitely."

Brandon and I thoroughly enjoyed the first part of our vacation. Life on a yacht as you cruise the Mediterranean Sea off the coast of France is not a bad way to spend a week. It was a week of firsts for me.

First time to France. First time on a yacht.

Brandon was sincere about making our relationship work. We were getting closer without any of the distractions of work or other obligations.

In Paris we were staying at the Le Bristol Hotel, one of Paris's finest 5-star hotels. As a bonus for me, Le Bristol was located in the fashion district. Brandon asked if I minded entertaining myself for a few hours while he worked out.

"I'm in Paris. The fashion district, no less. I suppose I can force myself to do a little shopping," I had responded with a sly smile. Credit card in hand I was off.

I was walking along Rue Du Faubourg-Saint Honore. Designer showrooms featuring clothes, cosmetics and furnishings from Dior, Chanel, Gucci, and avaunt guard exclusive Paris girl boutiques all beckoned me. Nowhere, not even the iconic department stores in Manhattan, were window decorations taken so seriously. Each shop window seemed more attractive than the last.

I stopped in front of Hermès to admire a hand rolled, hot pink, 36" x 36", silk scarf that would look fabulous worn as a blouse. It was 325 Euros. I figured that was about $445. Why not?, I thought to myself. I just received a substantial raise on top of an already great salary, and Brandon was paying for our vacation. I went into Hermès and exited twenty minutes later with the scarf and a few additional items.

I figured that Brandon should be done working out and probably back in our room showering. Brandon's impish smile and perfectly dimpled cheeks entered my stream of consciousness as I moved past Hermès. Dimpled cheeks on either side of two perfectly full lips located above his rugged chin. In all, a classically handsome face.

"Excusez-moi, s'il vous plaît," I heard a woman's voice say as she stepped around me.

"Excusez-moi," I replied apologetically, realizing I had stopped in the center of the busy sidewalk outside the Le Bristol Hotel. I had fantasy-walked my way back to the hotel.

As I entered the lobby, I was greeted by Fa-ron, the hotel's adorable Birman cat. He purred as I reached down to scratch his head. A bell hop offered to assist me with my shopping bags. I agreed, and we headed toward my room.

As I opened the door to the room, I was greeted by the cozy atmosphere established by the subtle colors of high-quality fabrics, vintage prints on the walls, and Louis XV-style furniture. Brandon made certain that we had all the comfort and serenity that a Paris 5-star hotel had to offer. The bell hop placed my bags on the couch as I asked. I gave him a tip. He thanked me and left.

I kicked my shoes off and padded over to the window and looked down onto the flower-filled courtyard in full bloom. I was once again appreciating the fact that I was on a luxurious vacation to France. The bathroom door opened and Brandon stepped out. He looked devilishly handsome in his charcoal gray dress slacks, a light blue dress shirt, red tie, and navy blue blazer. The same outfit, minus the tie, he had worn on our first dinner in New York at Tavern on the Green.

That night I had worn a black skirt and pink blouse. I had a similar skirt with me in my luggage. I decided I would pair it with the scarf-as-blouse that I had just purchased at Hermès.

"You look very handsome," I commented as I kissed Brandon on the cheek. "Why don't you go down to the Le Bar du Bristol for a drink while I shower and get dressed."

"Sounds like a good idea."

Brandon headed downstairs, and I got ready for dinner. I needed a little help from a YouTube video to figure out how to wear the scarf as a blouse, but it was worth it. I loved the way it fit me. I knew Brandon would as well. I grabbed my purse and headed to meet up with him.

As I stepped off the elevator into the lobby, I could see Brandon with a group of children playing with Fa-ron. "I would have taken you as a dog person," I said as I approached where Fa-ron was holding court with the human guests of Le Bristol.

Brandon turned toward me and his eyes widened.

"You look absolutely stunning, Ms. Sullivan," he said as he kissed me lightly on the cheek.

"Thank you. Just a little something I picked up today."

"Excellent choice. Shall we go?" asked Brandon as he took me by the hand.

"So, where are you escorting me to dinner Mr. Mitchell?"

"L'Abeille. Named in homage to Napoleon's favorite emblem, the bee, it is a French gastronomic restaurant that offers sophisticated cuisine in an enchanting atmosphere. It promises to reveal new emotions in aesthetics and flavors through hallmarks of culinary excellence including exceptional products and technique."

"How long did it take you to memorize that?" I asked playfully.

"Pardon?" Brandon replied in his best French accent.

"Just tell me, website or travel guide?"

Brandon laughed.

"Busted. L'Abeille's website. But I did already know it is a two Michelin-starred restaurant," he said.

"Good for you," I said, kissing him on the cheek again.

L'Abeille was located at lobby level of the Shangri-La hotel. As we entered L'Abeille we couldn't help but take in the history of the 1892 mansion that is the current day hotel and restaurant. Walking past the l'Escalier d'Honneur, the Staircase of Honour, we were in the very intimate restaurant. It opened onto a private garden that was pure luxury in one of the most expensive parts of Paris.

"This is lovely," I said.

"As are you," replied Brandon kissing my hand.

The host showed us to our table and left us with our menus. When our waiter came we ordered; both passing on frog and settling for seafood dishes. We ate, drank fine wine, and conversed easily. The setting was elegant and romantic.

"I know a great cafe along the Seine, not far from the Pont des Arts. Great dessert and then a short walk to a fabulous view," said Brandon after we finished dinner.

"Lead the way."

Brandon paid our check, and we were off for the next part of what was already a wonderful evening. After the most amazing crème brûlée, Brandon and I were gazing adoringly at the Pont des Arts and a panorama of Ile de la Cite, Notre Dame, the Louvre, and the city lights reflecting off the river Seine.

This is the most romantic moment of my life.

Brandon put his arms around me and drew me close. I breathed in the aroma of his cologne and let it dance in the night air. Every one of my senses was drawn to him as I became enveloped by his presence. He was intoxicating.

He gently lifted my chin. As we gazed into each other's eyes, he pressed his lips to mine. An older couple walked past us arm-in-arm and another stopped thirty yards from us to take in the view.

"Do you think that will be us in forty years?" Brandon asked.

"I hope so."

"Ashley, you are all I will ever need. I love you more than ever."

I looked deep into his eyes and became lost in their warmth and the genuine affection they held for me.

If the eyes truly are the window to the soul, then I was looking into the soul of a man's who love for me was true. There was no doubt Brandon Mitchell loved me. I could trust I was all that he would ever need. I felt exactly the same about him.

Chapter 27

The next morning we enjoyed breakfast out on the patio with our view of the Eiffel Tower. It was going to be our first stop on day one of our Paris tour. We'd have lunch in a lovely cafe and then take in the Louvre. We would round out our day with dinner and a cruise along the Seine.

A gentle breeze moved across the patio. It was a lovely autumn morning. The sky was clear and it would be a relatively warm day. Perfect for sight seeing.

"I am glad we took this little vacation," said Brandon as he added fresh jam to his toast.

"Me too. It has been good for us."

"This is what I want life to be for us all the time. Not a permanent vacation, but I want the way we feel toward each other, the way we are with each other, to always be like this," Brandon said, his voice earnest.

"If we want it to be, I see no reason that it can't be like this."

"I just want you to know how committed I am to that. How committed I am to you. Ashley, I never thought I would truly love a woman. To be in love with a woman. Let alone feel the deep love I do for you."

"I know. I saw it in your eyes last night."

"Window to the soul?"

"Something like that." I looked over at the Eiffel Tower. "Is it scary at the top?"

"You're not afraid of heights. So, no. It won't bother you. The view is spectacular. Also, very romantic. Great place to share a kiss."

"I'll keep that in mind."

"Please do."

We finished breakfast, showered, and dressed. We paused for a few minutes in the lobby to play with Fa-ron.

"Maybe we should get you a cat," I said to Brandon.

"Not if I have to clean the litter box."

"It's not that bad."

"I could have my maid do it."

"Do rich people always pay others to do the things they don't want to do themselves."

"Probably."

"I think it would be good for you to do it yourself. And feed kitty, bathe kitty, and take kitty to the vets."

"Wait a second. When did I actually agree to getting a cat?"

"Just musing out loud."

"I like this cat. But I can play with him and someone else is responsible for feeding and everything else. I'm not ready for that level of responsibility with a pet."

"Cats are pretty low maintenance."

"Still. Not ready."

I shrugged. I thought a pet would be good for Brandon, but I wasn't going to push the issue any further at the moment. We had Paris to see. We grabbed a cab and began our day.

The view from the Eiffel Tower was spectacular. It was romantic. It was also a great place to share a kiss. Or several.

The concierge at the hotel recommended a wonderful little cafe for lunch. It was off the beaten path and filled with neighborhood residents rather than tourists. It was perfect.

We only saw a fraction of the Louvre. We made plans to come back and see more on our next trip to France. The Mona Lisa was breathtaking. I didn't realize how much it would move me.

We ate dinner at a restaurant along the Seine and then took an evening river cruise. It was magical. It was reminiscent of the carriage ride Brandon and I had taken through Central Park. We sat close and snuggled and took in the City of Lights as we cruised along the Seine. We noted the sites along the river tour we wanted to visit the next day.

After the river cruise, we walked back along the Seine arm-in-arm. As we reached the Pont des Arts bridge, Brandon took me by the hand and led me onto the footbridge. The fence of the bridge had many locks on it.

Pont des Arts had long been known as the "Lover's Bridge." It was said that if you shared a kiss on the bridge that your love would last forever. A new tradition had been added to that. Now couples left a lock on the fence of the bridge with a love note before tossing the key into the Seine. The act was supposed to seal a couple's love forever.

Brandon removed a lock from his jacket pocket along with a notecard and pen. He scrolled his love for me on the card. He handed it to me. I wrote my love for him. We attached the note and lock to the fence. Brandon tossed the key into the Seine.

"I love you," he said.

"I love you."

"I don't want to take any chances," he said as he took me into his arms.

He kissed me. We shared our most sensual kiss on that bridge. A kiss to seal forever.

Do you want more Ashley and Brandon?
Turn the page for a preview of *Saying I Love You Forever*

Preview of Saying I Love You Forever

Prologue

I gasped for breath and fought back tears. I felt like I had been punched in the gut by the shocking news that we had just received. If it were true, it would shake the very foundation of the life Brandon and I were building together. In fact, it could quite possibly destroy any hopes we had of spending the rest of our lives together.

Gina Arlotti wanted more than to disrupt a wedding; she wanted to destroy Brandon's life. She wanted to deny me a life with him. Gina wanted to take everything we had for herself.

A week before, I had no idea who Gina Arlotti was. A week before, my life looked a lot different than it did in that moment. A week before, Brandon and I were celebrating the fourth anniversary of our first date and making plans for the future. A future threatened by Gina Arlotti's shocking news.

****

Chapter 1

Brandon Mitchell was a CEO with an almost rock star status. He held the title of most eligible bachelor and was considered one of the most handsome men in the world. Such a station in life allowed Brandon to date many beautiful women. Actresses, supermodels, even royalty. Ten years ago, one of those women had been Italian supermodel Gina Arlotti. It was a brief relationship Brandon had long forgotten.

There had been many women before and since Gina Arlotti. Four years ago, one of those women had been Ashley Sullivan. But Ashley was different from Gina and all the others. Brandon fell in love with her and their romance had blossomed. He was even planning on asking Ashley to marry him.

Brandon thought about his proposal as he drove his Aston Martin DB8 along the Pacific coast toward the Lusso Resort and Spa in Santa Barbara, California. The Lusso Resort was a special place for Brandon and Ashley. They had their first date at Francesca's restaurant located at Lusso's, followed by a long and romantic walk along the beach.

Brandon's daydreaming of their first date nearly caused him to clip the curb as he pulled up to Lusso's main entrance. Brandon removed his New York Yankees baseball cap and placed it on the passenger seat. He ran his fingers through his short, jet black hair. He left the Aston Martin with the valet and entered the hotel lobby.

Even dressed in faded jeans, a navy blue T-shirt, and an old pair of tennis sneakers, Brandon caught the attention of most of the women in the lobby. His six foot two inch athletic frame was pure muscle. His face was tanned and classically handsome. Brandon's lips were soft and full. The start of a five o shadow only added to his appeal.

Brandon crossed the lobby to Francesca's restaurant.

"Good afternoon, Mr. Mitchell," greeted the host.

"Good afternoon. I wanted to check on my reservation for this evening," said Brandon.

The host checked the reservation system. He gave a smile as he pulled up Brandon's reservation.

"Yes, everything looks to be in order." The host swiveled the computer screen him. Brandon looked over the reservation notes.

"Do you wish to make any changes?" asked Francesca's host.

"No. Everything looks good," replied Brandon.

"Excellent. We will make sure it is a perfect evening for you and Miss Sullivan."

"Thank you," said Brandon.

"Thank you, sir," said the host.

Brandon left Francesca's and headed to his suite in the resort. Ashley knew about dinner, but she had no idea what Brandon had planned. It was the fourth anniversary of their first date and Brandon wanted it to be a special evening.

As he opened the door to the suite, Brandon saw Ashley stretched out on a patio chair in shorts and a casual blouse. He never got over how great she looked without even trying. Brandon loved Ashley more than words could express. He never thought he would fall in love and want to spend a month with someone, let alone the rest of his life.

Ashley looked over at Brandon and smiled as he crossed the living room toward the open French doors. A warm breeze with a hint of the Pacific Ocean greeted Brandon as he moved toward the outside. Beyond the patio was the beach where they took their romantic stroll four years before and where they would share their special evening in just a few hours.

****

Chapter 2

I was already enjoying the fourth anniversary of our first date and it promised to get even better. The evening air was warm as Brandon led me along one of Lusso's oceanfront paths. It was in the general direction of Francesca's but not toward the restaurant entrance.

"I thought we were having dinner at Francesca's?" I asked.

"We are," replied Brandon. "With a little bit of a twist."

"A twist?"

"Yes. Be patient."

As we rounded the bend, I could see an elegantly set table for two on a private patio overlooking the Pacific Ocean. A waiter was standing next to the table.

"Good evening, Mr. Mitchell, Ms. Sullivan," greeted the waiter as we approached.

Brandon held out my chair for me and I sat. He then sat opposite me. The waiter poured us each a glass of our favorite red wine and left us with menus.

"This is absolutely lovely," I said.

The table had beautiful white linens and Francesca's fine place settings. The table and patio area was lit completely by candlelight. A string quartet appeared and sat off in the corner of the patio. They played softly in the background.

I glanced over at the quartet. I then took it all in. The ocean, the candlelight, the linens, the fine dinnerware, and, of course, Brandon. The love of my life. He was still my "Mr.

Handsome CEO." That is how my best friend Chelsea had often referred to Brandon when he was my celebrity crush.

Brandon's dark hair was neatly trimmed and perfectly combed in place. His tanned skin glowed in the candlelight. His gorgeous blue eyes twinkled with wonder and excitement. Brandon's smile was warm and every bit as captivating as I remembered it being when we first met.

Brandon was wearing one of his favorite double-breasted navy blue suits. He had a crisp white dress shirt and a blue tie to match the suit. I was wearing a black sleeveless evening gown with a deep neckline. Underneath, I wore a strapless black lace bra and matching panties.

"Brandon, sweetie, this all so wonderful."

"It is the fourth anniversary of our first date."

Brandon smiled broadly. I loved the way his mouth curled upward and formed two wonderful dimples. I also thought that he had the most perfect lips. Perfect for kissing.

"I'm just so glad to be here tonight. Of course, being anywhere with you is wonderful. We didn't have to fly cross country for our anniversary dinner," I said.

"We don't get here as much as I would like, so I figured this gave us a good excuse to take a little detour from our business trip to Los Angeles. Ashley, this is such a special place for us. That first evening together changed my life. It merits a grand celebration."

"Well, you have outdone yourself. I hope the after dinner celebration can live up to the dinner hype," I said with a seductive look as I took a sip of my wine.

"Oh, I can promise you that it will," replied Brandon.

"Very sure of yourself," I said.

"According to my girlfriend, I have a stellar track record."

"Yes. You do."

The waiter returned and took our order. We hadn't even bothered looking at our menus. We both ordered the Chicken Parmesan. It was what we always ordered when we came to Francesca's.

The string quartet played. The waiter refilled our wine glasses. A gentle breeze swept across the patio. Brandon and I were lost in each other's eyes. It was a wonderfully romantic evening.

"How do you think the Adele acquisition will go tomorrow?" I asked.

"I thought we agreed that we wouldn't talk business tonight," Brandon responded.

"I know. But I don't plan on doing much talking later. And the meeting is early in the morning."

"Ashley, look around you. Who cares about the acquisition of Adele?"

"Who cares? Well, you certainly are not sounding at all like the CEO that I know."

"I have far more important things on my mind tonight," said Brandon.

"Like what?" I asked.

"Like this Chicken Parm," said Brandon as the waiter arrived with our dinner.

"Very funny," I said.

"Anything else?" asked the waiter.

"No, thank you. Everything looks wonderful," replied Brandon to the waiter.

The waiter nodded and then retreated from the patio. Brandon cut into his chicken and took a bite. He had a satisfied look that he only truly got from great food, great wine, and spending time with me, and not necessarily in that order.

"Okay, now that you have experienced the rapture of delight from your first bite, let's chat a little about tomorrow," I pressed.

Jacqueline acquiring Adele was the biggest decision that Davenport Media had made in years. The news was all the buzz in the fashion industry. How could Brandon not want to discuss it?

"Okay. But just until we finish dinner. By the time we get to dessert, we are done with any talk of business until tomorrow morning. Agreed?"

"Agreed," I said.

"I think everything should go smoothly. Adele has a great staff. They will complement our Jacqueline staff very well. Having an office here will help us more effectively cover the west coast fashion world and related entertainment industry," said Brandon.

"I certainly hope that we will be keeping Lauren Caldwell, Ronald Vargas, and the social media staff," I said.

"Even though they tried to steal you away?"

Lauren Caldwell was the Vice President of Human Resources at Adele and Ronald Vargas was their Vice President of Business Development. A few years ago they had offered me a job at Adele to run their Digital and Social Media department. It was during a time when my future with Brandon was very much in doubt. The offer was extremely attractive. But Brandon followed me to California to win me back.

"Brandon, that was business. I stayed at Jacqueline. It should be water under the bridge. They are nice people and will be assets in running west coast operations," I stated.

"You actually don't need to convince me. They will be extremely valuable. They also seem rather excited about being part of Jacqueline. And, yes, they are both very nice," said Brandon.

"I think they realized that they seemed destined to remain in the number two spot, so now they get to be part of the number one fashion magazine," I commented.

"I guess the old adage of 'if you can't beat 'em, join 'em' rang true," agreed Brandon.

He took another bite of his dinner and savored the flavor in his mouth. Then he washed it down with some red wine. A nearly equal look of satisfaction came across his face. Then he spoke again.

"I've been doing a lot of thinking about what the Adele acquisition can mean for us. Not just the company, but us, personally. What would you think of moving our offices here to California? Most specifically, here to Santa Barbara?"

"Really? You are actually considering moving the company headquarters out of Manhattan?" I asked.

"We'd still have our Manhattan office and a lot of key staff would remain there. But there is a strong argument to be made that our biggest growth after the acquisition will be the entertainment fashion sector. Today's technology makes it possible for me to have my office pretty much anywhere," replied Brandon.

"Well, I love the idea. As much as I like Manhattan, I do miss Santa Barbara. Have you discussed this with your grandmother?"

Jacqueline Davenport was Brandon's maternal grandmother and the founder and President of Davenport Media and the namesake of its flagship entity, Jacqueline fashion magazine.

"I did raise the issue with her. She is on board as long as the company's involvement in the New York fashion industry and charitable events does not decline. I assured her that our presence in New York will be as strong as ever."

"What about your parents? I'm sure your mother isn't wild about the idea of you moving cross country," I said.

"No. But it's not like we all can't visit often. I mean, come on, they have a private jet at their use 24/7."

"Oh, and like you have ever flown commercial in your life," I teased.

"A few times in college, actually."

"Yeah, you have it rough. And I bet you flew first class."

"No comment," replied Brandon with a slight grin. "You know, if we do make the move, you could be more involved at the School of Arts."

I had graduated from the Davenport School of Arts at Santa Barbara University. I benefited greatly from the Davenport Scholarship fund and had volunteered on the fundraiser committee my senior year. I have donated faithfully to the fund since I started working, but I always wanted to be more involved.

"That would certainly be wonderful," I said.

We finished our dinner. The waiter cleared our dishes from the table. He then brought out a bottle of Francesca's finest champagne and two champagne flutes. He poured a sample in Brandon's glass. Brandon took a sip.

"Superb," Brandon remarked.

The waiter filled both of our glasses. He took our dessert order and then retreated to the kitchen.

"Okay, dinner is over. Per our agreement, no more discussion of business. The rest of the evening is just about us," Brandon said.

"I like focusing on us," I said.

"My favorite subject," said Brandon as he looked into my eyes. "Sip your champagne gently. You know how it can go to your head."

"So true," I said. I took a few sips of my champagne and giggled.

After a few more sips, I noticed something in the bottom of my glass. As Brandon saw me focusing on the object, he got up out of his chair and moved next to me. Then he bent down on one knee.

****

Order *Saying I Love You Forever* from your favorite bookseller.

Newsletter

Join my Newsletter and receive a Sweet Romance eBook story as my gift to you. You will also receive author updates, new release alerts, and exclusive contests and discounts. Free to Join. No Spam. Unsubscribe Anytime.

Join at elliejadamsauthor.com/newsletter

Books by Ellie J. Adams

For a complete list of my Sweet Romance books, visit:
www.elliejadamsauthor.com

About the Author

Ellie J. Adams's books have been downloaded over half-a-million times by readers around the world. She is a romantic at heart and likes her characters to find their Happily Ever After. Ellie's books offer moments of drama, humor, and heartache along the way. Her leading men are strong, but flawed, males, and the leading women are sweet, smart, and independent. Ellie writes sweet romance you can get swept up in and takes you away.

9 781952 748011